A monster lives in all of us.

My father abandoned me when I was an infant.
My friends have turned against me.
My uncle hates me.
The most powerful sapients in the world want me dead.
They all have one thing in common.
They think I'm turning into a monster.

I'm starting to worry they're right.

Over a thousand years, one man unlocks sapience—the ability to transform the imagined into reality. But not everyone believes sapience is a gift because this power blurs the lines between dreaming and waking, making it impossible to divide real life from nightmare and friend from enemy.

The most powerful of these sapients rule the world, sharing little in common save their venom for each other and lurid horror for Evan Burl —a sixteen-year-old imprisoned with twelve immortal orphans in a haunted castle surrounded by the bones of a forgotten city. Evan finds a letter that orders his execution—signed by his own father—that reveals Evan's latent supernatural talents. As Evan makes use of his new abilities, he loses his grasp on the physical world and fears he might be responsible for the string of gruesome deaths that have begun to plague the orphans.

With each passing day, Evan's waking world is fading into a mist of dreams, replaced by starless nightmares that just might be real. The fates of those who remain alive rest on whether Evan can regain his ability to tell dream from reality and save his friends from the sapients who would rather the world forget that these twelve orphans ever lived.

An

Backlash

Book

For Anna

Evan Burl and the Falling

Justin Blaney

"Justin Blaney's descriptive, yet punchy writing style is just one way Evan Burl and the Falling separates itself from the vast majority of young adult and fantasy writing being published today. With its intelligent and gripping storyline, relatable heroes, and highly-imagined villains this book captured my attention from the start. I can't wait to read what happens next."
Freya Hind

"The best fantasy book I've ever read"
Mitsy Princell

"Brilliant. I am recommending this book to all my friends"
Julia (from Amazon.com)

"Evan Burl is one of the most imaginative and creative (novels) I've read in a long time. Fans of fast-paced, action-packed fantasy will find a lot to love..."
Alyce Reese

"Well-crafted. Mysterious. Intriguing."
H.J. van der Klis

"I usually don't enjoy books of this genre... I'm really glad I took a chance. The characters were rich as was the story line. I couldn't put it down!!!"
Julie Weber

"Reading Evan Burl reminded me of how I felt when I read great books like Harry Potter or The Hunger Games for the first time."
Katie Zinda

"I read Evan Burl and the Falling when I was supposed to be working on my homework. That should speak for itself, it was a fantastic distraction from reality."
Jessie Crowther

"So much YA fiction has the same story with slightly different set pieces. Evan Burl, however, is truly creative."
Natasha (from Goodreads.com)

"I want more! It just isn't right that's over. Evan Burl is every bit as good as the top YA fiction out there right now, in my opinion, better. The characters are brilliant, each story line is captivating, the content is complex and unpredictable... I am intrigued to read more."
Bethany Canfield

"I'll never view a clear, blue sky the same! This book took ahold of my imagination and guided me through the forgotten hallways and secret rooms I've always dreamed of finding. A fantastic story about the burden of knowing one's destiny, and desperately trying to avoid it."
Eric Nienaber

"Wickedly complex villains so entertaining and terrifying they'll get under your skin and creep you out ... Evan Burl's world will fascinate you and leave you begging for more."
Mary Weber

"Really well written"
Angela Foster

"This eerie world and amazing cast of characters grabbed my heart from the first page and never let go. I can honestly say I would do anything to get an advance copy of Evan Burl's next chapter."
Natalie Medina

"The characters are awesome and the story is riveting."
Julianna Rickman

"I'm hooked. So many threads of greatness, I can't wait to see how the series ends."
Annie Biondi

"This book will take you on a fantastic odyssey that immerses your senses with riveting action ... you will see, hear, smell and feel Evan's dangerous journey of self-discovery, constantly in fear that something could rise up out of the ground beneath your chair and pull you into this strange world."
Hilary Hansen

"Justin Blaney creates a wonderful world of intrigue, mischief, and magic that comes alive through vivid storytelling. This is a struggle of good and evil at its finest ... it will have your mind on edge as you race to the end."
Kari Skinner

"This one is definitely a page turner! I must say this novel is much different than anything I have ever read."
Linda (from Goodreads.com)

"Rich, believable characters set in a captivating storyline that made me constantly anxious about what would come next. This story of hope and redemption will have you rooting for Evan to find the good within himself."
Marisa Loper

"A fantastic read."
Jestmesue (from Amazon.com)

"I am in love with this book"
Magen Bosarge

"My wife and I recently read this on a trip to the mountains near Seattle. Once we started, we couldn't put it down. The book will take you on an imaginative voyage that will rivet your attention."
Bob and Daphne

"Evan Burl and The Falling is a facination story of mystery and magic. Pay attention to the details and the scenes will come alive in your imagination. This Novel is such a new and different story. I was fascinated up until the very end."
Marsha Thaileen

"I have to say this book was amazing!! I seriously could not put it down ... an awesome present for those who are hard to buy for."
Melissa Willard

"This world is both incredible and terrifying at the same time"
Courtney Bax

Cast of Characters

Wards of Daemanhur
Xry Mazol
Yesler
Ballard

Orphans of Daemanhur
Evan Burl
Henrietta
Haller
Little Saye
Anabelle
Lucy
Pearl
Parkrose
Gertrude
Roxhill
Othella
Vashion
Ravenna

The Amadeus family
Terillium
Mercer
Anastasia
Claire

Other Characters
Cevo – *Chancellor of El Qir*
Mahalelel – *Vice Regent of El Qir*
Dravus – *Delivery Master*

The Leuschi Sea

Holler Bay
Bridlemile
Yarrow Point
Kenton
Deception Pass
Zenon
Leone
Daemanhur
Kerns
Irving Beach
Diana's Pond
Vernon
Healy Heights
Russell
Sabin
Oth
Per
Ka Tirret
Hamlin Fork
Parkrose
Aitzen Fork
Nortga
Bloodwood
Kenora
Geldon
Bailey Hill
Quader
Sullivans Gulch
Mauss
Hayward
Westmoreland
Clyde Hills
Dunlap
Gilman
Horg
Bitter Lakes
Eastmoreland
Mox
Glenfair
Harlow
Alameda
Creswell
Greenwood
Knight
Nickerson River
Mt. Buckman
The Kar River
Cal Young
Ravenna
Sellwood Moreland
Lorane
Wisto
Montclaire Hospital
Hilly
McArter
al Creek

Vol. One
Monsters

One

I found myself in a kingdom of stars and clouds.

Endless. Deadly. Blue as blood.

Stretching without blemish from one side of the world to the other, the sky was perfect but for one single inky speck.

If anyone was watching, they might have wondered if I merely napped on a pillow of thin air.

But it was nothing so pleasant.

This was a falling.

For what felt like hours, the whole world seemed frozen below me. Except for the wind, everything lay silent. It seemed as if I could stay up there forever. It was beautiful really, if I ignored the fact that I was hurtling toward the ground at a speed that would turn my bones to gravel upon impact.

I didn't even feel sick to my stomach—until the last thirty seconds.

First, the rolling mountains and hills lumbered toward me like big bullies begging for a fight.

Then houses and barns popped out of the ground, grasping hands from a fresh grave pulling me down into the earth where I belong.

Ten seconds later, what seemed like a bit of lint stuck to my eyelash transformed into a living human, far below. Then more. Dozens. Hundreds of people. Working, eating, anything but looking up to see me plummeting through the sky.

Another ten seconds—far too soon—and the whole world rushed up at a speed that turned my stomach to acid.

The last hundred feet were the real test.

Gulping one last lungful of air, I realized in that moment that I was less brave and more foolish than I could possibly have imagined.

And right before the end, I closed my eyes.

Like I always do.

Two

I woke with a gasp to the sound of men arguing.

I lay on my side in a bed of crackly brown leaves, each one large enough to wrap around my body like a cape. Rolling onto my stomach, I crawled under a sprawling rhododendron and stared through the foliage in the direction of the voices.

Two men passed through the outer wall of the East Gatehouse, under the trio of raised portcullises that were not supposed to be open. They led a grimacing horse and groaning cart that barely cleared the stone arch. I crouched lower.

"You can't hide forever," my uncle bellowed from somewhere in the darkness. "I know you stole it!"

The moon hovered high in the sky. I wondered how long I'd been out. Something bulged in my pocket. I pulled out a leather-bound book. My Uncle Mazol was going to beat me for this, but I couldn't remember stealing it. I could only read a few words, and those words were scorched in my mind, making my stomach twist each time I reimagined seeing them appear on the old pages. Then there was the dream. It played over and over. Falling. Falling. Falling. It always ended the same. Eyes clenched shut. Bones to gravel. Dust to dust.

I watched the men shift down the overgrown road, stepping over an endless web of roots, whacking the tangles with a machete. Their eyes never resting long on the path but always darting up at the three and four level brick skeletons of a city that rose on either side. The broken, lifeless buildings leaned over the alley; like their last breath was a sigh; like they might, if given a proper shove, touch in the middle and turn the alley into a tunnel. Their horse whinnied and tried to turn back for the gates, but one of the men—a towering, bulging figure—pulled her reigns and forced her on toward the western tip of the city. The jungle had long ago reclaimed this forgotten space between the walls. Nothing is more patient than the jungle. In time, it takes back the land stolen from it, when there are no humans remaining to beat it into submission.

The men drew close now. They squeezed the cart around a banyan tree that had staked its claim across the porches of two buildings and half the road. In ten years, I'd never seen anyone except my uncle and cousin inside the city gates. Deliveries from Queen Anne were dropped in the gatehouse, never inside the walls. Could I still be dreaming, finally seeing what came after the falling?

Lantern light flashed in a window behind me. My uncle was close, but I couldn't take my eyes off the men—one twice as tall and five times as large around as the other. The giant's skin was ebony, like men I'd heard stories about who lived in the great deserts over the mountains. The short one wore a porcelain mask that gleamed pearl in the moonlight; his skin so pale, it was nearly as white as the mask. Both men wore riveted brown leather and canvas with boots up to their knees and belts so thick I thought they might have been used to harness elephants.

I heard my uncle's footsteps pounding the floorboards. "Burl!" I pictured the lasher he hung above the mantle in his study, the round, stone walled room on the sixth level of the castle. Peering through the trees and above broken buildings at the castle's hulking shadow, I tried to picture where his study was. A few sparks glimmered orange in the gloom, one of them belonging to the fire in Mazol's study where the lasher grew hot. I wondered if I could make the belt disappear just by thinking it. I wondered if I could make Mazol disappear too.

The castle's tallest towers, silhouetted against a bloody ocean sky, rose even higher than the king of all trees: the two hundred foot baliza. No matter where I hid, it always felt as if the castle might fall on me. Its constant presence sucked the air from my lungs. Yet it was my home, if only because Mazol kept the food locked up in its pantries. The endless halls, the numberless rooms, the nickel and iron walkways, the alabaster tiles, the marble and glass walls, the unsearchable secrets, all drew me in like a salivating, toothy smile. The castle, Daemanhur, was a singular making of man that the jungle could not prevail against. Perhaps because the castle was alive too. It stretched on and on—a fungus that sprawled a little more each year, constantly added to, expanded and refortified over untold centuries. The baliza tree may be the king of all jungle plants, but Daemanhur was king of the jungle.

And the castle would save me from my uncle. I'd dissolve into the maze, like another of its countless occupants—rats, cockroaches, scorpions, spiders, hornets, shadows—only to emerge when I could no longer stand the hunger. By then, my uncle's head would be cooled. Maybe the belt's leather too.

The cart creaked to a stop, ten feet from where I hid.

"How scary could Evan Burl really be?" the giant said. "He's only ten-years-old."

"He ain't dangerous."

"Everyone in Queen Anne says it's worse inside these walls than out in them jungles."

"We'll be a smart bit more comfy in that big old castle than rotting in a dungeon."

"You shouldn't have poisoned her. Had a nice gig, we did. Now we have to take up with this Mazol and his haunted Daemanhur castle."

"It ain't haunted."

"A hundred years ago, everyone who lived in this city vanished."

The short man's eyes darted across the murky windows. "Do you think some of their souls is floating around in there?"

"Where did they all go?" The giant stared in my direction. I held my breath. His eyes narrowed, like he saw me. Then, he turned away. "This place is evil."

A crow, with wings longer than I was tall, flew overhead, cawing. Landing on branch that hung out over the road, he watched us with lidless, burning red eyes.

"It was just the plague," the masked man said.

"That or something from the jungle found its way in here."

"A lot of somethings."

More crows joined the first. They pecked and cawed at each other, fighting for the best position from which to swoop down on us if one of us looked like we might not fight back too hard.

The giant, leaning down to the other man, lowered his voice, "The old Miller man was whispering last week about a grim beast that lives up here."

I shuddered. Uncle Mazol tells me stories about a monster living in the castle. He says it only comes out when I'm sleeping. He says everyone has a monster hiding inside. That sometimes, if you're not careful, the horror finds his way out.

"Well I'm gonna rest pretty," the short one said. "Find me a right soft cot to sleep on tonight. Might even take up painting with all the free time we got coming. Just mind you keep that big iron portcullis shut tight, and we got nothing to worry about."

The growl of a jungle cat cut through the darkness from the direction of the gate.

"You did shut the gate right?"

"Said *you* were gonna," the giant said.

My uncle stepped out from the building, his wrinkled old face cast with flickering shadows from the carriage lantern. I edged back into the undergrowth. He stared at the open gate.

"Was just telling Ballard to shut it," the short man said.

"You better hope no beast took notice."

The giant jogged to the wall, his feet pounding the ground with thuds that made my teeth chatter.

"Yesler, where's the boy?" Mazol said.

Chains rattled. The first portcullis slammed down.

"I... uh... " Yesler's head tipped back as he stared up in the sky. "You see that?"

"What?"

"A flash of light."

Mazol frowned. "It's time then."

"For what?"

"They're coming."

Lightning split the sky. Thunder rolled. With a patter, fat rain drops began to fall, growing stronger and faster. Suddenly cold, I pulled my thin shirt around me. Wind whisked down the alley and rushed through the trees.

I stared up; rain stung my skin.

A murky shape crashed through the tree canopy, cracking and snapping branches. I shielded my face from a pelting of dust and debris as the object smashed into the mud in the center of the street. The flock of crows took to the air, cawing and circling above us.

I squinted in the dim light. A casket. Cracked and dented; built of rusty engraved iron, bronze and gummed wood; the carved side panels were lined with gears, smeared with grease, and covered in cobwebs. My uncle produced a three-tooth key and twisted it inside the lock. The gears spun to life. The lid jerked open with a clank and hiss. The men leaned forward, lanterns held high; their faces turned all to eyes.

I crept closer, tracing along the trunk of a banyan tree. I couldn't quite see inside the casket. The rain poured down, masking the noise of my shuffling feet.

"What happens next?" Yesler said.

"I ain't rightly sure," my uncle said.

A few low branches jutted out above me. Jumping, I swung up to a low limb that extended over the men then crawled until the branch began to sag from my weight.

Gasping, I covered my mouth.

A girl.

"She alive?" Ballard said.

"You think he'd go through all that trouble to send us a stiff?"

I crept further. The branch sagged lower. The bark was slick from rain. I slipped, but managed to swing back on top, showering the three men with dust.

The girl, about seventeen-years-old, wore thick, wire-rimmed glasses. Her lily skin shimmered in the pelting rain and twilight; her roughly cut raven hair fell just past her chin. I'd seen pictures of girls before, but they were clumsy sketches compared to the real thing. Like a painted cloud can't convey the feeling of flight. And this girl, she was close enough to touch. I felt her in my bones.

Uncle Mazol inspected a silver tag hanging from an onyx anklet above her right foot. "Hen-ri-et-ta."

Another crack of lightening filled the sky.

"That'll be the next one."

"How many are coming?"

"Eleven." Mazol gazed up, shielding his face from the rain. His eyes focused on me. "I've been looking for you."

I scooted back. My feet tangled. I slipped and fell, landing with a soggy splash on my back in the mud at Mazol's feet.

Three

Mazel twisted bony fingers around my wrist.

I ripped my arm away, jumped to my feet, and elbowed him in the nose. Dashing away, I heard my uncle yell, "Grab him!"

I looked back. The flash of lantern light lit their faces; a trickle of blood ran down Mazol's chin. I charged down a thickly overgrown alley. Their boots splashed behind me. Curses echoed out fainter and fainter, ringing over the pouring rain as the men collided with branches and stepped in potholes only I knew to avoid. I darted around a dragonhornet nest the size of an ox cart that hung next to a swinging hotel sign. A few bites from dragonhornets might make Mazol forget about the book I'd stolen.

I turned again, entering a part of the city that was so overgrown, almost no light reached the jungle floor. I felt my way along using the wall as a guide. Faintly at first, I heard something that sounded like crying. The sound grew louder. I moved toward the sound, stumbling on a wooden crate. I lifted the object, discovering it was another casket, smaller than the last. I held it to my ear.

A baby.

I fumbled with the clasp.

Behind me, a long, deep growl.

I froze; turned. Nothing, until my eyes traced upward.

Two rows of white fangs hung in the twilight above me. The hiss of rank, hot breath rolled from the beast's mouth. I stumbled backward. Claws swiped past my face. My back hit the wall. The beast lunged at me. I dove to the pavement, rolled over, tucked the chest under my arm and ran. Crashing through the brush behind me, the jungle cat chased.

I reached the fields of longgrass that lay between the city and the castle. No trees grew within a hundred feet of Daemanhur, like the plants were smart enough not to get too close. The beast flew over my head, pouncing forty feet in a single jump. A million heads of grass twice as tall as me swayed in the wind,. I could only see a foot in any direction.

I moved slowly, pushing the stiff green blades aside with each step. Behind me, rustling. Something whooshed past me on my right. I jumped back. A branch snapped under my foot. A few feet away, a low growl rumbled. I ran, dashing out of the grass into the paved courtyard that led to the castle's steps just as my uncle and the others appeared on the other side of the clearing.

I sprinted across the courtyard. They moved to cut me off. My uncle grinned. The cat jumped over my head, landing between us.

My uncle's grin vanished as he stumbled backward. "You let a Black Leopardi inside the courtyard?"

The giant slid the ax from a sling across his back. I turned around and ran for the castle, tracing along the wall back into the longgrass below the tallest tower. I rounded a corner and collided with my cousin Pike.

"What's going on?" Pike said.

"Come with me." I pulled him along behind me.

"Where'd you get that chest?"

"No time to explain."

The baby cried. Pike, snatching the chest, put his ear to it.

I grabbed it back. "We've gotta get out of sight. Quick!"

"What'd you do this time?"

I peered up at the tower that rose above us. Three hundred feet. Daemanhur's tallest tower. "Nice night for a climb."

"It's pouring rain."

I shrugged, ripped a stand of longgrass from a pile of straw at the base of the tower, tied it through the iron work of the casket, and slung it around my neck. I tested my foot's grip on the first ledge. "You coming?"

Gaps and ledges lined the wall of the tower all the way to the top, but I'd never climbed it in the rain.

"Let's just hide in the castle."

"Why, you scared?"

The giant cat screeched. Pike's eyes lit. Lanterns flashed against the wall of the castle. I flattened, trying to stay in the shadows.

Mazol yelled, "Found anything?"

"Foot prints," said Yesler.

I whispered to Pike, "Mazol's gonna whip me."

Pike craned his neck. "Who's that other voice?"

I began to climb. "I'll tell if you come up with me."

Pike peered into the darkness for another moment before following me. I explained about the two men and the girl in the casket. About fifty feet up, I stopped to watch two lantern lights dancing below us.

"How long you reckon he lasted against that Black Leopardi?" Pike said.

"That giant's as big as a horned elephant. Had a wicked ax. Might actually have a chance."

"What was it like? Seeing a girl for real."

I smiled. "Even prettier than the pictures."

"Does she have a name?"

"Henrietta."

We went quiet—the kind of silence I imagined would fill the moments after finding a chest of buried gold.

"And you're sure she's alive?" Pike said after a while. "I mean, do you think she's gonna stay? Hey, maybe she'll be my girlfriend."

"I saw her first."

"So she's yours, is she?"

"Didn't say that. Henri's just—"

"It's Henri now? You two must be closer than I realized."

"Shut up. She's too old for you anyway."

I stared out on the world as we climbed higher and higher. Daemanhur sits on a cliff's edge, high above the Leschi Sea which fills the northern horizon. A hundred foot wall encircles the courtyard, with houses and shops and passages built inside it. The wall runs close to the castle on the uphill, western side and stretches for nearly a mile down the slopes to the east in the direction of the harbor and a docktown called Queen Anne where a few hundred shipmen and their families live. That city was dying too. Mazol said it used to be home to ten thousand, long before I was born. But the jungles were growing more dangerous. Every week, more people left on north-bound ships and never returned.

Soon, Queen Anne would be like Daemanhur's forgotten city. Thousands of people might have lived inside the walls around our castle at one point, but Mazol said they all left a long time ago. Then he told me to leave him alone, and I didn't see him for hours.

A creek runs under the wall next to the smaller castle gate and passes through the abandoned city. It keeps the lake full year round, but most of the fish are too bony to eat. The creek runs out the lower side of the city, joining a large river just above Queen Anne. That's where the deliveries come from. An armored car pulled by eight huge horses and a band of hired guards brings us the supplies we need every week. The guards smell like beer and body odor and they swear a lot—but the one who's in charge is different. Dravus. He talks to me sometimes, while they're unloading the carts in the East Gatehouse. Dravus has been asking me to let him inside the walls. He said he wants to see the city. I haven't yet; Mazol said no one's allowed, but I might sneak him in someday. Dravus said he'll teach me magic tricks, maybe even my letters.

I thought about the book and the few words I understood. I wondered if Pike would read it to me. I wondered if I wanted him to know what it said.

It took another half hour for us to reach the top. Crawling over the eaves, we scampered up the ancient clay tiles to the roof ridge, placing our weight slowly as to not slip. Sitting on the ridge, we caught our breath. I pulled the chest off my shoulder.

Pike pointed at words engraved above the lock. "Rosling Corporation, Since 845"

"What do you think it means?"

"Maybe that's what they're called," Pike said. "Roslings."

I wondered if Henri had ever been to a city. Traded in a marketplace. Sailed on a ship. Maybe she could tell me what life was like outside the walls. I traced my fingers along the ice cold, rough-edged ironwork. "Do you think we could have come to the castle in caskets like these?"

"It's possible, I suppose."

"I've never seen any pictures or heard anything about caskets falling from the sky."

Pike eyed the chest in my hands. "I don't think it's normal."

"What if everything in the pictures is made up? Do you think there are other cities? What if we're the only people alive?

"There's Queen Anne."

"What if that's the only city left?"

"Where do the ships come from then?"

"I don't know, but I mean, doesn't it bother you? Everything we need is delivered to the gatehouse each week. Why can't we go to town and buy it ourselves?"

"You wouldn't survive outside the walls for five minutes."

"The runners do."

"They're trained. Got armor and a whole caravan and proper protection."

"But still, don't you wonder if this is real? I mean, we could be dreaming right now and not even know it."

"We ain't dreaming."

"How do you know?"

"I'm two years older than you. That's how."

I slid the book from my pocket, stooping over to keep off the rain.

Pike leaned toward me. "What's that?"

"This is why your father's gonna whip me."

He held out his finger to touch it. "Is it real?"

"Not sure."

"Imagine if we sold it? We'd be rich."

"I'm not trading it."

"Why'd you steal it then?"

"I don't remember stealing it."

Pike raised an eyebrow at me.

"There's something in here... I think Mazol's afraid that I might read it." The words ran through my mind, burned into my skull. I tried to ignore them.

Pike tried to grab it away from me. "You don't know your letters."

"I know my name." And a few other words. Like monster. I tucked the book under my belt and stared out into the fog of rain and mist. The moon appeared in a hole in the clouds, disappeared again before I spoke again. "Do you ever wonder where you fit in?"

"Like, what I want to be when I grow up?"

"If the whole world is a huge puzzle, where does your piece fit?"

"I don't know... far as I can see, I'm probably staying, help my father run Daemanhur. At least we're safe from the jungle here."

"I want my life to matter. I want to help people."

"Then help people."

"It's not that simple."

"Why not?"

"Because you have a father."

"What's that got to do with anything?"

"If I had a father, he'd show me how to be a good person."

"My father helps you."

"He wishes it was just the two of you."

"I don't think so."

I paused, the words from the book burning the insides of my eyes. "It's more than that. Remember the story Mazol tells. About how the castle's haunted?"

"About the shadow who roams the halls? He just trying to scare us."

"I heard those two men talking about it. Said people in town knew the story too. That people are afraid of coming up here. That's why we never get no visitors."

"We don't get no visitors because of the jungles."

"But what if there really is a monster living here? Mazol said the monster strangled my mother."

"Think we'd've spotted it by now."

"Unless..." I stared at the book.

"We should go," Pike said. "Father's gonna be burning angry."

"You're the *son*. You won't get in trouble."

"I'll tell him I didn't see you. Do you have enough food in the Elusian to stay hidden for a while?"

My eyes drifted to the corner of two roof peaks where a trap door was hidden. It led to a room I called the Elusian, an attic hidden in the rafters of the castle that Mazol didn't know about. "What if that's where the monster hides?"

"What're you talking about?"

I thrust the book into Pike's hands. "I don't think Mazol was making up stories about shadows."

Pike flipped through the pages, shielding it from the rain. Most were blank, except the first few.

I leaned over his shoulder. "Can you make it out?"

He studied a line, his lips moving a little. My heart beat so loud I wondered if Pike could hear.

"Well?" I said.

"I'm working on it." A moment later, he folded the book shut.

"What?" I said.

Jumping up, he slipped a little on the wet tiles. I reached out to steady him, but he flinched at my touch. His arm trembled.

"What is it?" I said.

He stared into the masked sky above the crashing waves far below. "You don't want to know."

"It's about me."

He turned away.

"From my parents, isn't it?" I said. "I saw my name. I saw the word... monster."

His eyes met mine. "I'll read it. But you ain't gonna like what you hear."

Four

Pike held the book close to his face, tracing his fingers along the letters as he read.

"Salve Xry Mazol,

"Until today, I never realized how foolish it was to allow Evan Burl to live.

"I had hoped, of course, that he might slowly grow strong, at a pace that matched his ability to handle the increasing power. And then, in time, he would have carried on in my place, keeping sapience in check, ensuring no one abused the power for their own gain.

"Of course, it was always possible the boy was only a minor sapient, capable of little more than a street magician. But alas, I fear now that he is neither a minor sapient nor capable of handling the sapience that soon will be thrust on him.

"Rather, I now believe it's highly probable he will become the most powerful sapient this world has ever known. Far stronger than me, or any of the three Cultures. If this is true, and because of the unique circumstances that surround the boy (partially due to my tinkering, I admit) it's likely he will grow not just deadly, but pure evil.

"I'm submitting the boy's blood for a test, a process that will reveal who, or what, he really is. This is very advanced stuff, difficult to get right. Therefore, I expect the results of this test will take some time. In fact, the boy may come of age before I can contact you again.

"Unless you hear from me, go through with the plan as I've previously instructed, with one exception. You will have to be much more aggressive now. The Spider alone may not be enough. If you have the ember, as I expect you do, that should save you. I would demand that you kill him now, but I still hold out hope that I'm wrong. Sometimes I meddle too much. Sometimes it's better to let the game play out. By the time the code in this letter reads zero, we'll know the truth, one way or another."

Pike stopped reading and scanned me. I wasn't sure if he was worried about how I'd react, or if he was afraid of what I might do to him. I stared out over the mournful dead city; trees growing out of the tops of buildings and in the streets and the strangling vines wrapped around the bones of all that was left behind by the ones who lived here long ago. I traced my eyes along the circle of longgrass around the castle, thinking about how nothing grew within a hundred feet of Daemanhur's foundations. What were the plants so scared of? The castle? Or the darkness that lived inside it? "What's the Spider?" I said.

He shook his head, turning to the page.

"Is there a surer sign of our changing times than this? Terillium Amadeus, afraid. Of a child, no less.

"He may appear to be a normal boy while he's young, but when he comes of age you will not recognize the monster Evan Burl becomes. You will watch the evil grow in him during his last year. And watch him carefully, because he must be stopped before too much strength resides inside him.

"If things go ill, and if the boy survives, remember this: no one will be spared. Not after the falling.

"Our only hope is that I'm wrong.

"Fortunatos and good luck, Terillium."

"6 years, 11 days until the falling."

A long silence followed. I thought about the dream. The falling. My bones turning to dust. Maybe, at the end of the falling, the part when I always close my eyes, maybe that's when Evan Burl dies and the terror is born. Maybe the monster is already inside me. Growing. Maybe he only comes out when I'm asleep. Maybe that's when the beasts come out to play.

Pike seemed to read my mind. "Father's just trying to scare you. He must have known you would find the book."

"The man who wrote this, Terillium, I think he's my father."

Pike put the book into his pocket. "We better get going."

"That's mine," I said, grabbing at it, but my foot slipped and I fell backward, pulling him with me. We slid down the pitch, bringing a few loose tiles with us. I scrambled for a grip, but every tile I touched broke loose. My hand caught on a nail just high enough to get my fingers around. My body swung sideways as I pulled Pike away from the roof edge. Spreading my legs and arms, I managed to support my weight without knocking any more tiles loose.

After a few heavy breaths, I said, "Almost forgot we're three hundred feet above the ground." I risked a glance down at the waving field of longgrass, an emerald ocean, but bone-crushing hard. Pike's body shook, but I was stone steady. I was convinced that if I ever needed to, I'd learn to fly. Birds learn to fly by jumping from their nests. Why couldn't I? Maybe that's what happens in my dreams right after I close my eyes. I learn to fly. Maybe I never hit the ground.

Pike breathed out. Laughed one strange 'ha' that was humorless. "You're going to kill me someday."

"Yeah," I said, echoing his fake laugh. "You might be right." Inside I thought about what monsters do. They kill.

"Let's go." Shifting, I put my knee on the tile, but it was too much weight and the tile broke loose. My leg slipped out from under me and I hit the roof. Three more tiles broke free. Pike tried to stop me, but he fell too. Our hands clasped together, but I couldn't stop sliding. Our bodies rolled over the edge of the roof. The leather book caught in the eave. Letting go of his hand, I wrapped my fingers around a beam just in time. Pike caught the board next to me. We dangled in the air.

"I'm slipping," he cried.

I tried to catch my feet on a window ledge but wasn't quite tall enough to reach. I watched Pike's fingers slip off the wet clay and was just able to grab him with one hand. Groaning from the strain, I felt my fingers slipping. I heard something above us, sliding down the roof. A baby cried. The chest. I knew in that instant I would not be able to save them both.

The chest toppled over the side.

I felt Pike's fingers slipping from mine. My eyes locked with his. Then he was gone, plunged into the fog below. My fingers grasped at nothingness, as if I expected to pluck Pike from the night air. The casket whooshed past. I clenched at the grass sling, grasping it at the last possible moment. It swung beneath me like a clock's pendulum, smashing through the glass window in the topmost room of the tower. My hand slipped off the eve as the chest clanked onto the wood deck.

Was this the falling? Or a dream?

I saw a vision of a salty ocean shore and a cottage. Smoke rose from the chimney. Someone ringing the bell, calling me to come to dinner.

Then I was drawn back to the tower, to the night. For a moment, I thought I was flying. This is how birds learn to fly, they fall first. I felt like I could hover in the air as long as I like. But this is not a dream. I'm just an orphan, and orphans cannot fly.

Five

Five years later

"I'll kill myself if I have to stay here one more day," Henri said, sobbing into my shoulder.

"I'll hang myself from the tower's rafters like Little Saye did last night."

We hid in a pantry; empty shelves lined the wall and the smell of flour and sour milk lurked in the air like an almost forgotten memory. My stomach churned. Even the faintest smell of food was unbearable.

"Make us disappear," she said, dropping the *r* like she always did. Henri spoke different than the others. "I can't take it anymore. Please, make us disappear."

I squeezed her tight in my arms. She couldn't really mean it. Only death lay outside the city walls. Worse creatures than my uncle and his two hired men lived out there. Wild animals, swallowing their prey while it still breathed, hoarding it inside their bellies until they got hungry enough to begin consumption—sometimes weeks later. Packs of dogs ate orphans like us one finger at a time. In that dismal and endless jungle, even the plants would turn on us, digesting our bodies slowly in pools of gooey sap beneath snapping shells disguised as man-sized flowers and leaves. And if we survived the animals and the killer jungle plants, we'd be hunted down by maneaters or a pack of Shades or a giant so monstrous he'd make my uncle's hired axe, Ballard, seem harmless as Little Saye.

No one survives the jungle. Not without hired swords and armor and transport. Not the Roslings. Not Mazol. Not even Ballard on his own. We were prisoners—all of us—more afraid of running away than captivity.

So we escaped inside our heads. All of us did. And I was the best of us all. I taught Henri to come with me into my dreams. We stayed up late, long after my uncle allowed us to stop working, talking about the lives we imagined. When I wasn't having nightmares of falling, I imagined living in a cottage on the beach with a father who loved me. Fantasy was the only way I managed reality.

I'd developed other ways of escaping reality too. A few stupid magic tricks I'd learned from Dravus, a tiny man with thick bushy side burns who delivered shale to the castle every Saturday morning. Henri was too old to be much impressed, though she always appreciated my effort. But the other Roslings—what we called the girls who fell from the sky the day Pike died—squealed and giggled no matter how stupid my tricks were.

Reality always caught up with us. This was about to be one of those moments. My uncle searched for us, possessing the supernatural sense of a predator. It was only a matter of time.

I pictured the passage outside, where my uncle lurked. A small curved hall led to the castle's towering entrance hall where eight passages split off to more passages which led to more rooms and more passages and stairs and halls and doors until you were lost in the endless puzzle known as Daemanhur. The arteries, great passages along the outside walls of the castle, were lined with arched glass windows, thirty feet tall and ten feet wide. Crystal chandeliers hung from the ceilings throughout the castle, each with mounts for dozens of candles. The ebony and alabaster floors were carved into a maze of vines, flowers, and trees.

Henri put her ear to the door. Mazol was getting closer. I imagined pulling a flower from behind my back, or a bit of stale bread from Henri's pocket, but after what happened to Little Saye last night—with what waited for us on the other side of the door—those tricks weren't up to the task.

"Please Evan," Henri begged, tugging at my hands as if... as if trying to force them to work magic. "We could do it. We could run away together."

Henri didn't know what she was asking for. The book I stole from my uncle told me my future: the most evil and powerful sapient the world had ever known. Henri had never seen the book, and I'd make sure she never did. I hugged her tight to my side, imagining real magic in my fingertips. Sapience. That's what the book called it. In my mind, it was easy. Just wave my hand in the air and we were both gone. Sapience was more than magic. Beyond simple tricks. With sapience, even the jungle couldn't stop us. I could make a new world just by thinking it. My dreams would become reality.

I pushed those thoughts away. My only hope was that the book was wrong about me—that I wasn't a sapient. That my nightmares were just that. Dreams. That there wasn't really a falling. That I didn't become a nightmare whenever I fell asleep.

Henri cried louder—tears soaked my shirt where she lay against my chest. Her body shivered like a cornered mouse. I tucked a few strands of her choppy hair behind the black glasses she'd worn since the day I first saw her.

"Shhh," I whispered. "They'll hear you."

Didn't Mazol care at all about Little Saye? Didn't he care that we might all be scared after what happened to her? The floor vibrated from the pounding of feet in the hall.

Henri gasped. "I couldn't help eating."

"Shhh. I know."

"I'm so hungry." She twisted the black anklet on her right leg, like she always did when she was scared. All the Roslings had one, each with the broken base of an hourglass hanging from it. Impossible to remove, and somehow, as the Roslings got older it grew larger.

"I'm hungry too. We're all hungry."

"But it hurts. It hurts so bad."

Sometimes we ate grass or tree bark just to make the pain go away for a little while, even though we knew it only made it worse later. The jungle plants that had overtaken the abandoned city weren't edible. Nothing that came near the castle was. Even the fish, bony as they were, had stopped swimming in our lake long ago. One day, when I was swimming in the lake, I rose to the surface to find I was surrounded by floating carcasses. That was three years ago.

"Just keep telling yourself the hunger's only in your head," I said, "remember?"

Mazol said only eleven Roslings were supposed to fall the day Pike died. But in the end, twelve came. One of them was extra, or Mazol was wrong about the number. They were special. We discovered it shortly after they arrived. Burns, cuts, broken bones, nothing harmed them. They could feel pain, just like me, but cuts or bruises, no matter how bad, usually healed in an hour. Except for feeling sick with hunger, they didn't even need to eat. That's how Henri could go days, sometimes weeks, without food. Somehow, she never grew gaunt from hunger like you'd expect.

And the other thing about Henri, the thing that was either extraordinarily wonderful or unnervingly creepy—she wasn't growing any older. The first time I saw her I figured she was about seventeen. About the age a girl is when she's as tall as an adult, but still thin in the hips and shoulders—that's how I imagine teenage girls from the pictures I've seen. And now, five years later, Henri looks exactly the same as the first day I saw her. Sometimes, and I try not to think about it if I can help it, I imagine she's actually much older than she appears. If she's not growing any older, how can any of us know how old she really is? And then, other times, she behaves like she's as young as the other Roslings—like her mind is confused about how old she's supposed to be. We used to think that she and the other Roslings were immortal.

Then Little Saye died.

"I don't know if I can do this." She wiped her face with the sleeve of her faded yellow dress. All the Roslings wore dresses like Henri's, made from floral bedsheets with pockets on each thigh right above the hem.

In the hall, someone flung open a door and it crashed into the wall. Dust fell from the ceiling, stinging my eyes.

"They're almost here," Henri whispered, her voice breaking. "They're going to find us."

I imagined the punishment that was coming for both of us. No food for a day? A double shift of work? A belting?

"Please, Evan. I know you can do it. Make us disappear."

Why did she keep saying that? Could she know about sapience?

Real sapience.

For a moment my heart beat faster—sapience would have given me the power to keep Little Saye from dying. I could have saved Pike the night we fell from the tower.

No. I shook my head. I can't let the book be right about me. I can't be sapient.

"Take us where it's safe," she whispered.

I hit the floor with my fist. "Nowhere is safe."

"Far away," she insisted. "There must be some place, far away from here."

"We'd have to cross the jungles."

"Not if you made us disappear."

"That's just a dream." I turned away.

"Sapience." She said it so quietly her voice was almost drowned out by the thudding inside my head.

"What did you say?"

"Sapience," she repeated. It came out as barely more than a hiss.

The monster inside me smiled. Short for breath, I imagined invisible hands wrapping around my neck. "You're confusing our dreams for what's real. We can't really escape. That's only games we play."

"Will you try?"

"It's just tricks Henri. I can't do real... sapience." The thing inside me said, *liar*.

"It is real."

"Stop saying that." I put my hands over my ears, trying to block out the voice of the monster inside me. And it was Dravus too. He told me just yesterday that I was special. That I could do sapience. Why did he say that yesterday, after all these years of saying nothing? Just hours before Little Saye died?

"I've always believed it's real." Her whispers rolled inside me like shouting.

"Why?" I said, "Why do you believe?"

She paused. I held my breath.

"Because you're not a bad person..." she said. "You'll only become a monster if you choose to become one."

"You've seen the book, haven't you?"—the book I couldn't remember stealing from my uncle. The book that lodged in the eaves of the castle's tallest tower the night Pike died. It was a year before I climbed back up to get it, sure I wouldn't find it there. Sure it was destroyed. But the book was there, just like I'd left it. Like I'd left it there a moment earlier and was pretending a whole year had passed.

She nodded. My face tingled; my head wasn't getting enough blood.

Voices echoed in the hall.

Henri was so close I could hear her eyes blink.

"It says I'm becoming a monster."

"It says your father could be wrong about you," she said.

"But if I have sapience, that proves he's right."

She put her hand on my thudding chest. "You can be a sapient *and* a good person."

Footsteps echoed down the hall. I waited for them to pass. "My father doesn't think so. That's why he left —"

"You don't know that."

"—he realized I wasn't worth sticking around for." I smoothed an imaginary crease in my pants.

"Don't say that."

"That's why Mazol hates me too. He knows what I'm becoming."

"He hates you because of Pike."

"Only a monster would let Pike die."

"You're not evil and you never will be," she whispered so loudly it came out like a growl.

"What if I can't tell what's real anymore?"

"You can always do what is right."

More footsteps outside the door. "Wait," said a low voice. "Heard something."

The door handle rattled.

Henri gasped.

In the key hole, a single, ugly eye appeared.

"Look at this," said the voice. Uncle Mazol. I imagined him grinning at Ballard and Yesler, the other two wards, or Warts as the Roslings and I called them, who kept us working day and night on steam operated clanker machines. "Found our dear little Henrietta."

The eye dissolved. Feet scuffled outside.

"Evan," Henri begged. Her face was almost touching mine. "Please, just try."

The door rattled again. Banging.

I rubbed my eyes, suddenly itchy and wet. "I'll just hurt you."

"I believe in you."

The air charged with static. I pulled at the collar of my ragged shirt. It seemed like everything in the tiny pantry pressed down on me.

I heard metal clinking. Mazol, trying different keys.

"Hurry, Evan. I know you can do it." Henri's voice was different. Stronger.

Mazol yelled from the hall. "Ballard, get over here and help me with this lock!"

I clenched my eyes shut as a message grew stronger inside me. Insistent. Impossible to ignore.

Help her.

A single thought moved in a way I'd never felt before, from my mind to a place deep in my gut. Or was it the nightmare trying to escape?

I lifted my hand, fingers trembling.

On the other side of the door, something slipped into the lock. But it didn't turn. More keys rattled.

My hand hung in the air—as if acting on instinct—waiting for the cue to begin. My cheeks flushed, suddenly I felt thankful it was so dark. Maybe Henri hadn't noticed.

Dust sparkled in a sliver of light shining through the key hole. Like watching a thousand fireflies waltzing. The particles slowed to a stop, hanging frozen in time, watching to see what happened next.

My hand began to move.

It felt like—sapience.

My mind cleared. The constant pain in my leg was gone. In the dim light I saw Henri's eyebrows rise with anticipation. Watching my fingers move, I felt they belonged to someone else. They seemed about to strike an invisible match in the air, and then they stopped.

What were they waiting for?

With a crash, splinters of wood shattered against my face. Henri screamed. A fist burst through the door.

Light streaked through dust-clogged air.

fire

A melon-size fist broke through the solid koa-wood door like it was made of match sticks.

Five cracked-stone fingers unclenched, ripping away what was left of the door. The jamb and part of the wall disappeared into a cloud of dust.

Light flooded in, drowning us. I blinked, swearing at myself for waiting that last second. Three shadows rose, silhouetted against the towering windows behind them. The only adults I'd ever really known: Uncle Mazol, Ballard, and Yesler. The Warts.

Ballard reached through the dust, yanking Henri by the hair. She dissolved into the light, screaming.

I jumped up, plunging blindly after her. Pain shot through my leg, a constant reminder of the night I fell off the tower with Pike. Ballard's free hand became a wall in front of me. I made out the outline of Henri's body crumpled at Mazol's feet.

I fought to reach Henri. Ballard caught me by the neck. Uncle Mazol yanked Henri's arm. Twisting it behind her back, he forced Henri to her feet.

"You canis." Mazol shook her. "Made us miss a full half-day of processing."

She sobbed.

Mazol squeezed her mouth. "This if for your own good, can't you see that?"

I pried at Ballard's fingers but might as well have been trying to rip roots from the ground. "You're hurting her!"

Yesler backhanded me across the face. The sting of his gaudy rings cut my cheek. I tasted blood.

"That's enough." My uncle was particular about who got to beat me and when. "All of you, follow me."

Mazol dragged Henri by the arm. She tripped to keep up. Ballard pulled me along by the back of my shirt. My bad leg screamed with every step. Yesler followed last; unblinking, eyes grinning through his porcelain mask. As we turned toward the castle's domed entrance hall, I caught a glimpse into a room I hadn't seen in years.

For a moment, I was taken back to playing with toys, pretending to fight off bad guys with sticks and Mazol smiling like a man who enjoyed kids but didn't know how to show it. Now Mazol was the bad guy.

We stopped in the center of a towering room. Carved marble staircases swept up both sides of the room to a balcony. The front wall was lined with windows and two large doors that led to the stairs and courtyard. The windows were covered with velvet curtains that allowed only cracks of sun to pass around their edges. Dozens of statues and tables and bookshelves covered in white dust sheets surrounded us like ghosts.

Mazol released Henri and began to search under sheets. "Someone find me a stool."

Yesler took a turn around Henri. I imagined him inspecting a defective clanker in much the same way. Slipping a knife slowly from his belt, he licked the blade then pressed it to her throat. "Like stealing food? Skipping out on work all day?" Yesler glanced in Mazol's direction. He pressed the dagger deeper into Henri's skin. A trickle of blood ran down the edge. Henri squirmed and cried out. He pushed harder.

"Does it hurt?"

I lunged at him, but Ballard yanked me back.

Pulling a dusty white sheet off a set of brightly painted tables, Mazol looked over his shoulder. "Cut it out."

Yesler put his knife away but didn't turn away from Henri. Mazol dragged a burnt orange stool across the mosaic tile floor. The screech seemed to linger long after the stool had stopped moving.

"Uncle Mazol," I said, fighting against Ballard's grip.

He ignored me.

"I stole the food."

Mazol waved his hand at me for silence. Yesler pulled Henri to the stool.

"She didn't do anything wrong!"

There was barely room for both of Henri's feet on the stool. "Stand here until sun-up. You'll have plenty of time to think about your selfishness."

"A full day—" I said.

"If you make it that long," Mazol continued, "I won't be giving you no lashes for your thievery."

I wriggled away from Ballard. "Let me do it instead."

"The gimp wants to be a hero, does he?" Mazol said.

"You can't stand for five minutes without your crutch," Yesler said.

"I can do it."

"You're needed in the Caldroen," Mazol said. "Just what exactly do you think will happen to us if we don't get our work done each week? The deliveries will stop coming. Then we'll be immanis worse than hungry."

An enormous mechanized clanker arrived on the cart with Ballard and Yesler the day I fell from the tower. A replacement for one of the forty-eight steam operated machines that had since become our sole reason for living. The Caldroen is where we spend most of our waking hours now — a six-floor, glass-domed, hollow tower at the center of the castle — where sooty iron walkways and clankers and spiral staircases cling to the walls like spider webs.

"You'll get your chance, gimp," Yesler said "Still got yours coming." He turned to Henri and whispered, "We could have had some fun with that shiv, you and I."

He ran his finger along the scar where he cut her neck. Like the other Roslings, Henri healed fast. Yesler wiped the last drop of blood off her neck and licked his finger.

"She was starving!" I yelled.

"It's only in her head," Mazol said.

"We wouldn't have to steal if you fed us more."

"Enough! If I catch you sneaking in here tonight, I'll double her time." He turned to Henri. "And if you so much as take one step off this stool, you'll get a lash for every hour remaining until sunup. I expect you to show up for work tomorrow morning all the brighter. Clear?"

She nodded weakly. As Mazol walked from the room, I found Henri's eyes. Shrouded statues towered around her. Tears dried in patchwork on her blushed cheeks. Her glasses, crooked. Dirty rags hung about her skinny body.

"I'll get you out of this," I whispered. "I'll make it right —"

Behind me, Mazol laughed. I felt like a fool.

"What do you think a worthless gimp like you can do to make anything right?" Mazol stopped in the threshold, staring back at us. I said nothing.

"All you do is make life miserable. Why do you think I'm stuck taking care of you? Your own father couldn't even stand to have you around."

The beast inside told me to tear his head off. I stepped toward Mazol, my fist clenched.

He grinned. "Got something to say, gimp?"

I ground my teeth. He'd just take it out on Henri. "Nothing."

"That's what I thought." He waved away a giant red fly that landed on his forehead.

I turned back to Henri. There was something about her, a look in her eyes, like a puzzle I couldn't fit together.

Mazol's voice droned on in the back of my mind. "...what you should be doing is thinking about how you're gonna make up for all the lost work you've caused. If we don't get our orders done, none of us is gonna eat..."

She must have been frightened, furious, even disappointed I had let her down. But she only looked guilty. I hung my head as Ballard started to pull me from the room. Glancing back, I kept eye contact with Henri for as long as I could, limping along as she grew smaller and smaller behind me.

I was about to grant Henri's wish—to make her disappear—into the shadows. Yesler offered a stick to me with a smile. "Here gimp. Left your cane back in the closet didn't you?"

I eyed him and held out my hand for the cane. He tossed it across the room. Yesler put out his foot as I stepped forward. My left knee cracked against the stone as I hit the floor.

"Watch your step, gimp." He caught up with Mazol in the hall. "Who gets to give Henri the beating if she falls off the stool?"

"You're sick, know that?" Mazol said.

"How about we make the gimp do it?" Yesler said.

"You hear that, gimp?" Mazol said over his shoulder. "You're swinging the belt if she don't stay on that stool all night."

"Don't you think he's had enough?" Ballard said.

Yesler grinned. "It's perfect. Only way to keep him from helping her."

"You know the gimp," Mazol said. "Always trying to be a hero."

Ballard's heavy feet pounded the stone methodically as we walked away. Turning, Yesler took a long look back at Henri. "I hope she falls."

Seven

I didn't make a sound when Yeder took his belt to my back.

The buckle cut my skin, but even the crack of metal on bone faded under the crashing waves in my mind.

I sat on the front porch of my cottage by the sea. A ship bobbed in the distance, ready to take me to a new world across the ocean. And when the whip tried to cut through my dream, I heard only the sound of a wave breaking upon the rocks.

The lashes weren't for stealing food. I was being punished for climbing the tower with Pike five years ago. Every punishment went back to that. I started sneaking Dravus inside the gates four years ago—he taught me about science. Physics. How little changes can add up to the difference between life and death. A thousand seemingly inconsequential events caused us to fall just the way we did. A soft breeze. The turning of the earth. The way our bodies moved, and how we changed our paths through the air without even knowing it. The result was a ten foot distance between where we each landed.

Crack. The belt stung my skin. But it wasn't a lashing. Just a row of white towels whipping on a clothes line in the wind.

The night we fell, I hit a pile of longgrass. Broke a dozen bones. Dravus said my leg would never heal properly. Said I would have pain the rest of my life.

Pike wasn't so lucky.

He hit the cobblestone path. Dravus said a body can bounce six feet into the air after a fall like that. I've fallen hundreds of times in my dreams, but I've never kept my eyes open long enough to know if Dravus is right.

Crack.

"That's enough," a voice said. Ballard ripped the belt from Yesler's hand.

Yesler shrugged. "I was done anyway. Any more and he'd be worthless."

"The Caldroen," Mazol said. "Ten minutes."

Yesler added, "Don't be a hero. Just forget about Henri."

I heard Yesler and Mazol's footsteps disappear down a hall as Ballard untied my hands from the hook on the wall. I limped after them, wondering how I was going to save Henri without either of us getting caught. Ballard walked with me.

The Caldroen gets its name from the boiler that sits in the center and rises up four levels. At the base is a furnace with openings that looks like eyes and mouth. At 1550 degrees, it's hot enough to turn me to ash in seconds. The heat powers the boiler which sits on top: a tank of boiling water that makes steam for the clankers.

Our job is to keep all forty-eight clankers running—copper and iron beasts, they rattle and hiss and moan and creak and pop, caught in the web of platforms and walkways that hang from the Caldroen's walls. Pipes go in, and pipes go out. We don't know what the clankers do, but Mazol says it pays for food and supplies to run the orphanage.

Ballard and Yesler worked for a year to get them all working. They'd been out of operation for decades. I used to stare up at them, my eyes wide at shiny copper and spinning gears and levers and gauges and pipes. The fun didn't last long. Not once I realized I'd be working those clankers from sunup until sundown, six days a week.

Ballard offered an arm to lean on as I limped down the hall. He was funny like that—might hold you down under Yesler's whip in the morning and sneak you a sip of Mazol's beer an hour later when no one was looking—as if that made up for anything.

Under his other arm, Ballard carried one of the smaller chests that the Rosling infants were found in. Instead of transporting Roslings, now the chests carried the stuff we processed day and night. I wondered if even Ballard knew what's inside them.

He gestured to a bench. "Don't run off. I'll be right back."

He set the chest next to where I sat. I realized the door that led to the entrance hall was just a few feet away. Henri could hear me if I yelled her name. Was this a test? I focused on the door handle. It seemed to be calling me, begging me to open it. I limped across the hall. My fingers closed around the cool brass knob. I started to twist the handle, then stopped.

Henri would suffer even more if I was caught.

I returned to the bench and slumping down, focusing on the window in front of me. On the horizon, a ship turned into the harbor. Where was it coming from? Was there a little chest on that ship bound to be delivered to our gatehouse, filled with who-knows-what? Dravus made deliveries every Sunday morning. The chests had to come from somewhere. Why not across the ocean?

Dravus's armored guards, runners they were called, earn more money than the mayor of Queen Anne. They had to be fearless, ruthless and talented with a spear. Intelligence wasn't required. Of course, runners don't much live past thirty. If they survive that long, they paint their skin green as a mark of honor. But the jungle gets them all in the end, even the greenskins. Because the jungle is patient. She always wins.

When the runners are unloading and resting up for the return to Queen Anne, I sneak Dravus into the city. For about an hour each Sunday, he teaches me whatever I want to know. I thought about last Sunday. Dravus seemed standoffish, like he knew something bad was about to happen. Could he have known about Little Saye? As I stared at the South Gatehouse, I saw movement. I stepped to the window. Pearl stood at the gates. She threw her weight against the latch that released the weighted locks. Chains shook. The doors swung open.

Six armored warhorses and a fortified cart flew through, screeching to a halt by the grim iron lamppost that stands lonely in the center of the courtyard. Pearl jumped back, barely avoiding being crushed under the horses' hooves.

Three men jumped out of the cart, two of them greenskins. This was all wrong. They're supposed to come on Sunday. They're supposed to drop the goods in the gatehouse. Where's Dravus?

The men took turns with a jug of brown liquid as they pulled canvas sacks off the cart and stacked them on the road. One man, at least 7 feet tall with arms as big around as my legs, threw his jug into the air as another shattered it with a whip. Another pulled a second jug from inside the cart and took a long drink.

Pearl cut a wide path around them, but the greenskin with a thick red beard spotted her. She headed for the longgrass. The man dropped a sack to the ground and staggered after her. He yelled something. Pearl changed direction. The other two cut her off. She tried to shove past them, but they pushed her back. The red bearded man caught her. She screamed.

I limped toward the nearest door.

Ballard appeared, holding a steaming loaf of banana bread. "Look what I found."

My stomach turned over from the sweet smell. I kept moving.

Ballard took a bite. "Aren't you hungry?"

I passed him.

"Where are you going?" he said.

I shoved open the door to the courtyard. Stumbling toward Pearl, I picked up speed—pushing the pain from my mind.

"Whaz your name, litt'l girl?"

Another yanked her arm. "Be a good girl now."

The bearded man covered Pearl's mouth, stifling her screams. She bit his thumb. He yanked back, cursing. He never saw me coming. I barreled into him. We crashed into the cart. He hit his head on the cart's iron wheel and fell motionless to the ground.

Huge sticky arms wrapped around me from behind. I smelled sweat and beer and pipeweed. A fist flew at my face. I ducked, wriggling free. One of the men lost his balance and fell. He rolled onto his back. I jumped on his chest. The first thing he saw was my fist crushing his nose. I got in four punches before the third man pulled me back by my hair. I swung my arms, but he held me easily out of reach. The other two men rose to their feet. One grabbed a shovel from the cart.

"Hold him still for me."

He aimed at my face and swung.

I winced.

A crash. I opened my eyes and saw the man with the shovel flying through the air. The one holding me by the hair let go. I spun around. Ballard stood behind me. He caught the other two men and knocked them together.

The bearded man ran toward the gate. The other two pulled themselves up, managing to jump into the cart. Circling around, they whipped the horses into a gallop.

The bearded man yelled, "You can forget 'bout the rest of this delivery." Blood dripped from his face where I knocked him into the cart.

He jumped on the cart as it sped by. "Dravus will hear about this. No one from Queen Anne will ever come here again."

Pearl ran into the castle. I rolled onto my back, moaning. I heard Ballard slam the gate shut. A flock of ravens circled overhead, cawing.

A moment later, Ballard's huge face appeared over me, still chewing a bite of the banana bread. "What were you thinking, coming out here all alone?"

"I had to do something... she was going to die."

Ballard leaned down and lifted me into his arms. I winced when he touched my back.

"Oh she was, was she?" He smiled.

"I should have done more."

"Don't you worry about that now. Let's get you inside."

I shut my eyes. In my mind, I watch Yesler, not Pearl, being attacked by the runners. But I have to stop imagining things that aren't real. If I'm not careful, I might start to lose track of what's my imagination, and what isn't.

Eight

Sometimes, after dreaming about the falling, I wake in a hallway I don't remember falling asleep in.

Or a room I've not been in for months. Henri said it's just sleepwalking.

I found myself wishing I could make it happen to me today. I wanted to fall asleep, wake in the entrance hall with Henri, and pull her down from the chair, into my arms. Into my dreams. To wake in the bedroom we shared, cuddled under a blanket whispering secrets to each other until we were too tired to even mumble. To find ourselves in the cottage by the sea, to a place far away where we were safe, where we didn't have to work, where Little Saye was alive again.

But I am in the Caldroen. And this is not a dream.

Everywhere I looked, sunken red eyes stared back at me—eyes ringed by pale and grief veined skin, sucked tightly around small boned children. As the Roslings worked the clankers, they choked back tears. Some gave in, sobbed a little, until one of the warts told them to shut it. Little Saye had departed us. Roslings aren't supposed to die. But could they be murdered?

Instead of crying, my jaw grew tight. My teeth set. My back stiffened. I watched the Warts for signs of their guilt. I thought about Dravus, how he acted last Sunday. What did he know?

Mazol didn't mention the incident with the runners, not after whispering about it with Ballard. It must have cost Mazol a fortune, the runners left with almost all the supplies. Why wasn't Mazol more angry with me? They all watched me. The Warts. The Roslings. Their eyes darted away whenever I looked, but I knew they were watching.

I thought the day would never die, until finally, long after the sun had retired, I stumbled to my room and fell face first onto the pile of blankets. The smell of Henri filled my senses. A tear rolled from my eye. The room felt cold without her. A fly buzzed somewhere nearby. Like my mind, it refused rest. I rolled to my side, wincing. Hugging my shoulders, I imagined Henri's arms around me, but I couldn't dream away the image of her standing in that unlit room all alone.

Waves crashed on a beach in my mind, beckoning me to join them on the shore. Would we wake tomorrow to find another body tapping against the window? Sitting up, I found a tiny wooden doll beside my bed and the sack of trinkets Dravus discovered in the castle. I dumped the contents of the sack into my palm. A few pieces of twine, a silver chain, and seven onyx iron cast models with clasps, like bracelet charms. Each had the word *rubric* engraved on the base.

"Be careful with these." Dravus placed them in my hands, clasping his old fingers over mind tight. "And don't ever let Mazol or the Warts know you have them."

Something about the rubrics made me feel butterflies whenever they touched my skin. I rubbed each between my thumb and my forefinger for a moment: a flat star with six points, a lotus flower, a tiny elephant with its trunk raised, a model clanker, an hourglass vialus with whirling smoke inside, a crescent moon, and a human skull. Little Saye wore the lotus rubric the night she died, hanging from the thin silver chain around her neck. It was Dravus's idea; he said it might help with the nightmares she'd been having—the last thing he said to me before leaving Sunday morning. I remembered his words when we found Little Saye's body—'don't let Mazol find them'—and managed to slide the necklace off her just before Mazol found us.

I tucked the star, the twine, and the doll into my pocket, then grabbed a cane. I lifted myself up. Every muscle in my body begged me to lie back down. Peeking outside, I looked twice in both directions. I never felt alone here. The Warts had a way of appearing whenever and wherever I least expected it.

I limped down passage after passage, until I came to the entrance hall where Henri stood lonely on her stool. I stared at the door, confused. I thought I was going to see Pearl, to check on her after the attack, see how she was getting on with Little Saye gone. Crying came from the other side of the door. I began to turn the handle. Then, somewhere in the drab behind me, snickering. I thought of Yesler, hiding in the shadows, waiting to see if I went to Henri. The belt in his hand. I pulled back from the door.

I couldn't go to Henri. I couldn't.

I forced myself to move on. Turning to the left, I shuffled down a long passage. To the right, up a flight of stairs, to the left again. I tried to account for all my time that day. Had I fallen asleep, even for a moment? Was I ever alone? Just when Ballard left to get the bread. What if I'd fallen asleep? I might not have stopped the runners from attacking Pearl. I might not have woken until it was too late.

All day long I'd been wishing I could fall asleep, then wake somewhere new. I thought through each moment, but it was impossible to recall them with any precision. Time didn't pass in the Caldroen. Moments turned to days. Days turned to years. Remembering the life that passed in that cursed room was like pouring rain back into the sky.

My feet carried me to Pearl and Anabelle's door. On the other side, the sound of rustling bed sheets. I pushed the door. Anabelle lay on a four-post bed in the center of the long, sunless room.

I approached. Her eyes closed, she tossed, talking to herself. Her forehead was wet with sweat. I shook her. She lurched. Screamed.

I wrapped my arms around her. "It was just a dream."

She fought against me.

"It's me, Evan."

Finally she squeezed me tight. I stifled a cry from the pain in my back as her hands brushed my skin.

A voice from the shadows. "She's been doing that for half an hour."

I pulled back, staring into the blanket that enveloped the room. "Pearl?"

The ten-year-old girl glided ghostly out of the mist. "I tried to wake her."

"It's alright now." I helped Pearl climb into the bed. "Do you want to see a magic trick?"

Anabelle nodded, her eyes glossy cold, like she'd nearly run out of tears.

"I suppose." Pearl smiled, but it was cast in bronze. That was the best anyone could manage after Little Saye.

I pulled a bit of cloth from my pocket and lay it over my fist. Pausing for effect, I lifted the cloth dramatically.

"Nothing's there," Pearl said.

"Oh?" I checked my hand, turned it over. "I must have done it wrong. Let me see." I winked at Anabelle, placed the cloth back on my hand, peeked under it, then put my finger to my lips.

"Shhhh. You have to be very quiet for the magic to work." I waited another second then said, "You pull it off this time."

Pearl lifted the cloth up slowly, as if something underneath might bite her. In my open palm was the star, fastened to the twine, and the doll. Pearl snatched the doll and hugged it tight, and I slipped the bracelet onto Anabelle's wrist. They kissed me.

"Now time for bed."

Falling back, they pulled the bedsheets up to their chins. I smiled as widely as I could without making my face crack. "Keep that little star safe and it will keep the bad dreams away." Where had I heard that? Dravus?

She nodded, playing with the ebony metal star. It glowed with silvery brilliance.

"The star is cold," she said.

Tucking her in, I noticed a rash on her neck. "What's this?"

She scratched. "Don't know. Bug bite maybe."

"Does it hurt?"

"Just a little itchy."

My chest tightened. I kissed her on the forehead and went to the door.

"Tell me if it gets any worse?"

"I will," she said sleepily.

"Night."

Neither responded.

I shut the door, holding the handle so the latch wouldn't make a sound.

Where had I been all day? Was I sure I didn't fall asleep? Was I sure I didn't let the monster out? Images flooded my mind of Little Saye's body tapping against the window. And on her neck, a rash.

Nine

Sometimes I make the letter from my
father disappear, like the pages of that
little leather book get stuck together.

Or like they've been wiped clean. Then, the letter is back again, like it's been there all along. Like it was just hiding for a spell.

After visiting all the Roslings, I let my feet take me where they wanted for a while. Eyes drooping, I found myself turning down a narrow hall that sloped upward into the heart of the castle. My feet were worried. They were taking me to the Elusian—the one place Mazol and the Warts could never find me. The place where the book was hidden.

My feet wanted to know, would I find the letter if I looked tonight?

The sound of footsteps echoed behind me.

I stared back. Alone—at least, alone as I ever was in this place. Always lonely—never alone. How can you be truly alone if you have a terror living inside you? Rain echoed on the roof, tiny chanting voices or marching feet—that's what I must have heard. Just the rain.

Stepping inside the broom closet at the top of a long, steep stairwell—more of a ladder really—I shut the door and felt the back wall. A bronze switch protruded at the base. I stepped on it. A small door swung outward. Air whistled through the gap below the door behind me as wind whooshed past.

I had found nineteen hidden rooms in Daemanhur. Some were entered through fireplaces. Others, through the ceiling of the room below. A few, through furniture like towerclocks or false dressers. Entrance sometimes required codes or combinations or piano keys struck in just the right order. One of the trickiest was accessed by stepping inside a claw-foot tub, drawing the curtain and turning the hot faucet to the left. Instead of water squirting out, a door in the tile wall opened, barely large enough to crawl through.

But the Elusian was the best discovery of them all.

Long and tall, the room was capped by thick wooden trusses and beams. The only light came through high gable windows jutting out of both sides of the roof and a flickering, humming light I couldn't explain that hung from the wall—tiny red glowing tubes formed letters: the word *Elusian* in large script, and below it, smaller script, *Fine Spirits*. The room sealed perfectly from the rest of Daemanhur; Mazol wouldn't have heard me yelling if he stood in the closet I'd entered through. Equipped with a hidden firewood elevator, it was possible to stock wood from a small basement six floors below without carrying it through the castle. And there was a rickety ladder that led to the roof entrance I had intended to use the night Pike died.

Moonlight filtered through the windows. Water dripped from the ceiling into a dozen overflowing barrels and buckets around the room — an orchestra of rhythmic melody that made me feel slightly less lonely. On one wall, a ceiling height fireplace was stacked with wood. Another pile of logs sat near an overflowing barrel of water. I struck up the fire with flint and kindling.

On the far wall lurked a hutch. Inside, the book I stole from my uncle. Now that the book was so close, I wasn't sure I wanted to see anymore. The hutch — that chained animal — seemed to rattle on its feet like something dangerous hid inside — something that wanted to escape.

Again I heard footsteps. The door to the closet swung open. Hadn't I closed it? My eyes darted around the room, watching. Had one of the Roslings followed me up?

"Is anyone there?"

No answer. I clicked the door shut, locking both bolts this time.

Limping toward the oppressive hutch, I felt eyes watching from the dusky fog. All kinds of critters and insects called the Elusian home. The eyes I felt must be theirs. No one but Henri knew about this place. And Henri was still in the entrance hall, wasn't she? I imagined Henri and Mazol whispering after I left her this morning, her agreeing to spy on me in exchange for ending her punishment early and receiving a few mouthfuls of bread —

I shook my head. Stop imagining things.

Passing shelves and stacks of old things I'd collected over the years, I shuffled — a stalling, dreading sort of jaunt — toward the hutch where the book waited for me. An assortment of shoes, each with spikes sticking out the heel — I laughed when I'd found them, hundreds of pairs in several closets. What could they be for? Punching holes in the ground? Several boxes of inky drawings so realistic they looked like real people were trapped inside — I imagined they jumped off the page whenever I wasn't looking. My collection of books — almost the entire set of Natural History with 19 of 21 volumes about everything from anthropology to zoology. If I could find a way to sell them, I'd probably be richer than a Lictor.

I taught myself to read with those books; Dravus helped of course. Besides Dravus, those books were the only reason I knew anything about the outside world, though I wasn't convinced everything in them was real. Things like elk: large brown-skinned animals that grew racks of horns on their heads. Or snow: white fluffy stuff that fell from the clouds. The book even had drawings of clankers that flew through the sky like birds; clankers so huge people actually lived inside them.

I glanced at the black hutch in the corner. With every step it grew larger, shaking and rattling and groaning. Sounds echoed off the hardwood walls, unseen guests watching from the darkness. Would the book stop calling me if I made it wait long enough? Could I make it forget what was written inside the pages?

I examined what remained from my collection of toys, ninety-eight of them, if you counted each of the marbles separately. I used to have more than I could count, but Mazol sold them all long ago. Life-sized toy soldiers that shot oranges out of cannons, train engines you could ride that poured real smoke out of their stacks, and balls that bounced so high they could hit the ceiling in the great hall.

The first day I showed Henri around the castle, I gave her a knit doll that could talk. She laughed — probably because I was ten and she was practically an adult and I obviously had a crush on her. But she took the doll. It tilted its head up as she cradled it in her arms and said, "Mama." Looking back, I can't believe how much she put up with my make believe. Henri and I would pretend, or I would at least, that Little Saye was our baby. She was the one I'd carried up the tower the night Pike died.

Henri and I found Little Saye hanging from the rafters in the top of the great castle tower this morning. Mazol said she killed herself. Six-year-old Little Saye, covered with bruises. How did she get all those bruises?

If there was a murderer in the castle, the only suspect I could think of — besides the monster — was my uncle. I didn't want to believe he was bad. He was the only real family I had left. Then I remembered the look on Henri's face as I left her on the stool. Guilt. Maybe she was hiding something from me about Little Saye. Maybe Mazol was making her keep a secret.

My feet bumped into the base of the dirkwood hutch. I stared at the single, knob-less drawer at its center. A scorpion disappeared into the shadowed corner of one of the shelves. The keyhole seemed to transform into a fanged mouth.

"Feed me," the mouth said.

The key.

Reaching behind the hutch, I brushed aside cobwebs to find a long iron key with a dozen scrolled notches along one side. I pushed the key into the mouth. It snapped shut. Swallowed. Moaned.

Click.

So precise. So different from the clankers—oiled gears and mirror-polished cherrywood adorned the hutch. Like the masterwork of craftsman who woke up early every morning to sharpen their skills.

The drawer slid open. Inside the cherry-lined drawer was a single item.

The leather book.

I saw Pike's face again as he read the words to me. Then, his face as he fell from my grasp into the mist below. My chest blistered as I turned the brown leather book in my hands. It should have shown signs of wear from that year of weather on the roof—yet it was flawless. I breathed in the smell of pulp and cowhide, traced my hand down the spine, feeling every groove of embossment on the leather. Words of another language were stamped on the edges amidst a geometric pattern that seemed to have more meaning than I could ever hope to understand. Around the book was a thin leather cord, wound tight to keep the pages from running away.

I untied the strap, flipping slowly through the two hundred and nineteen perfectly white pages—the only blemish was that the first twenty or so pages appeared to have been torn out. The paper was made from flecks of fiber, its edges torn. Each page was one-of-a-kind in thickness and variation.

Holding my breath, I rubbed the first few together, making sure to pull them apart properly. Ink. Words. The letter.

I let out my breath, like one of Dravus's runners facing a night in the jungles alone. I limped across the room to the blaze, unable to resist the book's call. Slumping against the wall, I traced my finger along the scrawled black letters.

Salve Xry Mazol,
Until today, I never realized how foolish it was to allow Evan Burl to live.

When I reached the end, I stared at the countdown below my father's signature.

355 days, 12 hours, 47 minutes until the falling.

Yesterday, it read 356 days. Tomorrow it will read 354. The numbers were counting down to zero.

If the letter was true, I was a sapient, like Henri said in the closet. But it also meant the falling was coming in 355 days, when I would finally turn into a monster. If Mazol didn't lynch me first.

Falling, according to Natural History volume six: dishonored, disgraced, defeated, moral death. What kind of a beast would I become? A physical monster? Morally dead? I wanted to have faith like Henri — believe the parts I liked, the parts about being a sapient, and forget the parts about becoming the Disgraced One; but I couldn't. Either the whole letter was true, or none of it was.

I stared into the coals, watched Pike's hand slip from mine, watched him melt into the fog. Then I saw myself falling, my bones turning to dust as I struck the ground. And from the dust rose a shadow.

A bead of sap exploded and sparks landed on my leg. I had put in too much wood; the fire was getting hot. Someone could push me in if they wanted — but I was alone, wasn't I?

I thought of Henri, standing on the stool. Thirteen hours had passed. At least three more to go. For a terrible moment, I felt comfort at the thought of her standing there; wishing she was standing there instead of lurking around the castle doing Mazol's secret bidding. I pressed my hands against my skull, tried to push the stampede of thoughts away. The Roslings were starving. Why didn't the Warts feed us more? Where did all the money go? And the shipments of goods. Huge shipments of who knows what. We worked day and night on Mazol's clankers, and yet we never had enough. Those runners took off with the delivery that morning; now we had even less. Could we survive if the people in town believed the runners? And why didn't Mazol seem to care that I'd chased the runners off?

I squeezed the book until my knuckles went white. If I looked again, would I find another letter? Another clue? Nothing at all?

I started to flip through the pages then threw the book into an empty bucket. It tumbled over. Someone's presence grew cold behind me. Words in my ear. *Read it again.* I spun around. No one.

The footsteps. The feeling someone watched me from the darkness. The voice. Was this the monster?

Jumping up, I piled more wood on the bonfire. I tossed on a painting I'd stolen from Yesler and smiled as it went up in flames. I worked until my clothes were soaked with sweat and my muscles ached. As I threw the last log on, I nearly tumbled in myself. The flames licked up high above my head into the flue at the top of the ceiling-high fireplace.

I looked at the book, feeling its condemnation stare back. I used to hope my father would come for me. I used to watch the front gate for hours, sure he'd come if I waited just a minute longer. An hour longer. A year longer. He'd realize he was wrong. Eventually.

I lifted the book. Found the pages that held my father's letter and — before I realized what I was doing — ripped them out.

No, said the voice in my ear.

I crumpled the letter. Threw it on the blaze.

My shoulders straitened. My head felt a little more clear.

My eyes fell to the book.

I could throw the whole thing in. Just the flick of my wrist and I could be rid of it forever.

Yes, the voice said.

I watched my hand, as if it belonged to someone else, jerk toward the flames. But my fingers held tight; they didn't want to let go. My hand jerked again. My fingers pinched tighter.

Do it, said the voice. *You're going to regret this, but do it anyway.*

I threw the book, forcing my fingers to let it go.

The book landed on the logs, splaying open. The top few pages of the book lit. They seemed to resist the flames. The book fought for its life. But one by one, the pages curled up, edges glowing bright as coals.

I was angry. Guilty. Ecstatic.

I listened for the voice. Sweet silence. Had I really done it? Had I killed the nightmare?

I grinned. The letter was wrong about me. I wasn't a sapient. I was just an orphan.

My smile grew.

More of the pages caught fire. Black smoke billowed over me.

Tears ran down my cheeks.

I seized a poker. Pushing it into the inferno, something caught my eye. I poked the book with the iron tip. The burnt pages flipped. Something was there I'd never seen before.

Writing.

New words appeared, letter by letter, as if someone was writing them at that very moment. I squinted, trying to make out what the words said.

Urgent. Lectito statim.
Xry Mazol, I received the results of the test regarding Evan Burl —

Ten

Terillium

"The things you cannot live without will bring you to your knees," Cevo said.

"Nothing can extirpate me," I said.

"*Anything* can kill you, if you love it too much. The price of immortality is to love not."

He said these things the last time we talked. He wanted to keep me from getting too close. To keep me nimble. To help me make the hard call when times became murky.

He was right.

He was right about Evan Burl.

I've stood in platinum halls filled with kings lying prostrate before me. I've surmounted thrones as multitudes shouted my name. I've conquered snow-capped mountains, defeated oceans, vanquished heavens. The people of the world shout, "Terillium the Great," as I pass, then whisper under their breath, "Terillium the Unum," when they think I'm out of earshot.

And this boy, this Evan Burl, this Bête Noire could be my undoing. All because I thought the world might not survive without him. I'm still not sure it can.

Four hours until sunrise.

Time is up.

My armada's flagship, the thousand-ton barque Elandian, had lulled most of the 455 crewmen onboard to sleep hours ago.

At times like these, when all I have for company is my past, the faces come back.

Tonight, Evan Burl's mother lies in my arms.

For the thousandth time, I watch her suck her last few gasps of breath. Always the faces. They haunt me, crawling out of the abyss when I am weak.

I clench my eyes tight, bury the woman back from whence she came — the damp mines of my mind. I move on.

Build another wall.

Lock another door.

Dig another grave.

Bury another face.

Occidere alium diem.

My life had been reduced to a cast of routines, all to keep my secret guarded. All to keep the ones I loved secure.

I bid good night to the eight guards standing straight as masts outside my door. Brushed my teeth just inside the door so they could hear. Pulled the curtains shut. I managed only ten minutes of Un Voyage en Ballon before realizing I couldn't remember a thing I just read. And the author was supposed to be a pioneer in science fiction? Placing the leather strip back to where it was the night before, I laid the old tome on the nightstand. I dialed down the lantern next to the bed until its flame flickered out in a puff of smoke, then I rose silently and walked through the dullgloom to an adjacent room that contained a table, six chairs, a large chest, and no windows.

I shut the door silently, locked it with both the deadbolt and the hidden internal lock I'd installed myself. As I approached the chest, the lid lifted. A neatly stacked pile of bedclothes floated out, situating themselves on the table. I stepped inside the chest, turned to face the locked door and descended into the belly of the ship.

I sat at a small desk in a cramped room. Hundreds of well-worn hand tools surrounded me, hanging lonely and unused on every square inch of the walls. I clicked a round button inscribed with a sans-serif T in its center. A light hanging from a cord above the desk sprang to life. Unlike the ships' many lanterns and candles, this light hummed ever so faintly as it ebbed out warm, soft pulses through the large glass ball enclosing it.

Nothing put me at ease more quickly than the hum and flicker of electric resplendence, perhaps because I was one of only a few men in the world who had ever seen one. A gnat appeared out of the darkness, buzzing in a trancelike dance around the glow. I swatted the bug away; it dematerialized in a puff of smoke.

I scrawled a few words on a blank sheet of parchment.

Urgent. Lectito statim.
Xry Mazol, I received the results of Evan Burl's test today. The news is worse than I imagined possible. I fear for your safety.

But what to write next—execute Evan Burl? Or let the boy live?

Cevo would have a few choice words for me if he saw me now. Yet he was the reason I had to be so careful. I couldn't let Evan Burl fall into his hands.

I read Evan Burl's test results again — all eight words, if you counted the sender's name. It arrived that afternoon tied to the foot of a pigeon, confirming the worst of what I guessed about the boy. Normally, my genius for guessing correctly would have pleased me, but what I felt bordered on despondency.

I risked much in hiding Evan Burl. More still in leaving the Spider to Mazol's care. If Cevo discovered their location, if Evan Burl escaped, all would be lost.

I lifted a bracelet from the desk. I'd been working on it for months — a gift for my daughter — in case I didn't have much time left. She would be taller now. Would she smile when she saw me?

I tucked the bracelet into one of the long pockets of my worn leather pea coat. My daughter's face provided the resolve I'd been searching for. I scrawled the last few words onto the papyrus before me, read them back to myself, then pulled out a small leather book and copied the letter onto the first blank page.

Crumpling the original, I turned it to flame with a flick of my finger. As the paper transformed into heat and smoke, Evan's mother flashed through my mind again.

"This is best for him," I said. "Optimus quisque."

The chair screeched on the worn plank flooring as I stood. I stuffed the book into the same pocket as the bracelets and cleared my desk.

The message was sent. I felt lighter. Decisions are sometimes more difficult to make than to carry out.

I imagined my daughter, my little Bell, running up the plank to greet me, six months older than the last time I'd seen her. If the winds favor us, we could be home in a few days.

But the tome weighed heavy in my pocket. Would my daughter run to me if she knew what I'd just done? Non puto.

Eleven

Evan

The blaze roiled with hunger and heat.

The pages would soon be gone. I reached for a pair of tongs, but found none. I pushed the book with a poker, but could only shove it further into the inferno. I kicked the logs. The fire settled. The book fell deeper in.

I felt I might burst into flames myself from the heat, but I edged closer, shielding my face. I reached into the flames.

The hairs on my arms withered. My skin screamed. The last page caught. The book was too far. I ripped my hand back, dunking it into a barrel of water at my side.

I threw my weight against the bucket. Water sloshed out, but the barrel didn't budge. I splashed the flames. Steam billowed out, scalding my face. I put my shoulder against the barrel again. I managed to tip it on edge, but the base rolled away from me. The bucket tipped sideways. Water rushed out onto the floor.

Gritting my teeth, I reached into the flames again. Pain seared me. I willed myself to reach further. My finger brushed the book. My shirt caught fire. I jerked back. The sparks rushed up my sleeve. I yanked off the shirt and lunged at the blaze again, but my leg gave way. I collapsed.

Rolling onto my stomach, I watched a log fall on the book. The fire burst higher with the pop of exploding sap and a flurry of sparks. I shut my eyes. Too tired. In too much pain to move. The inferno's roar screamed inside my head.

In my mind, my eyes pierced the logs and smoke and flames. The book was right there. A few feet away—it might as well have been miles.

I imagined reaching out to pluck it from the flames. My hand grew hot. In my mind, I pushed my hand into the fire. Except it wasn't combustion. Just dancing lights and smoke. My fingers wrapped around the book. Dravus said I could do sapience. My father feared my power. Henri believed in me. They were all saying the same thing.

I only had to try.

The blaze shifted. I imagined lifting the book.

Then I opened my eyes.

My hand stretched toward the fire. Three feet beyond my reach, the book wobbled on the logs.

It rose out of the smoke.

Twelve

Evan

I froze, not daring to breathe.

My hand hovered. The weight of the book felt heavy in my empty grasp. I inched my hand away from the sparks. The book quivered, dropped. I jerked my hand up. The book flipped over, rose slowly back out of the flames. A wasp the size of my thumb buzzed passed my ear. It crawled up my cramping arm.

I tried to pull the book toward me again. Turning my palm up, I pulled my hand away from the combustion. The book wobbled and slowly moved toward me.

My arm shook. The book moved like cold molasses. I flexed my thumb to alleviate the cramping. The wasp stung me. My hand jerked. The book dropped. I managed to hold still, lifting again slowly. The book stabilized. Minutes seemed to pass. The book was almost beyond the fireplace.

Sweat rolled down my forehead into my stinging eyes. The cramping become too much. Reflexes took control. My fingers sprang open. The book fell. It landed on the hearth, just beyond the flames' reach.

Crawling forward on my elbows, I clenched the smoking book in my hand. My nose filled with the smell of ash, smoke, and burnt hair. My heart clanked inside my tin chest. I peeled back the leather cover.

Charcoal pages clung to the binding, smoking, burnt to the stitching. I made out a few letters, a shade darker than the charred paper on which they were written. Scanning, I found four words.

Execute the boy immediately.

Then another at the bottom of the page. A name.

Terillium.

My own father had ordered my execution.

Thirteen

Evan

I dreamed about falling again.

This time, I wasn't alone. Another speck on the horizon, too far away to recognize. I'd never fallen with anyone else before.

I woke to the sound of a rat gnawing the cuff of my pants. I sat up, knocking my head on a beam that ran from the roof to the floor. As I rubbed my forehead, last night rushed back. I had used sapience to pull the book from the fire.

I was a sapient.

Proof that the letter was right about me. Soon, my nightmares would become reality. And who would be waiting for me on the other side of the falling? My friends? My father?

Just me, the monster answered. *I'm all you've got now.*

Dawn grew in the gable windows. I found the book—wrapped in a scrap of linen—just how I left it last night before I passed out. I unfolded the wrappings, my hand searing with pain from the burns. Hadn't I read enough? Did I really want to inflict more pain on myself? The wrapping fell to the floor.

The book wasn't burned.

Hairs on the back of my neck rose. I flipped through the pages, each one perfect, like last night never happened. Even the letter I ripped out was back in its place.

Could I have dreamed it? Had I not used sapience?

Flipping to the page where the new letter had appeared, I found only blank paper. My shoulders relaxed. It was a dream. I wasn't a sapient. I wasn't a monster.

But then I saw my shirt on the floor: charred and damp. A puddle of water. An overturned barrel. I reached out to steady myself and felt the pain in my hand again.

I counted the pages, starting with Terillium's first letter. A few pages were stuck together. Pulling them apart, I found writing. The new letter. I clapped the book shut. My father's words ran through my mind.

Execute the boy immediately.

Taking a breath, I opened the book.

Urgent. Lectito statim.

Xry Mazol, I received the results of the test regarding Evan Burl. The news is even worse than I imagined possible. I fear for all of us.
Execute the boy immediately.

I stopped, read it again. My face went numb.

Do not delay or you, and many others, will surely die.
Fortunatos little brother,
Terillium

Collatio Tomi: Do not go to Cevo for help. I fear he would try to turn the boy for good, which is of course, impossible, and dangerous to anyone who tries. Evan Burl will become a monster—I am certain of that now. There is nothing you or Cevo or anyone else can do to stop it except to kill him while you still have the chance.

The book fell from my hands.

All this time I'd been fighting it. But I was a sapient. My father was right about me all along. What reason was there left to resist?

You can't resist your own fate, the nightmare inside me said.

But I'll hurt my friends. I'll have to run away to protect them from myself.

Then run away.

There's still time, isn't there? A year to be with the Roslings? A year to be with Henri? And what if I resisted using sapience? Stop sleeping. End the nightmares. Fight the monster for control of my mind. Maybe I could slow the countdown.

My eyes drifted to the bottom of the page.

3 days, 16 hours, 52 minutes until the falling.

I read it again. It was supposed to say 355 days. Not 3.

Now I had only three days.

I knew you'd throw it in the fire, if I pretended to be scared, the monster said. *And now look what you've done. You accelerated the falling by using sapience. My time is coming soon.*

Laughter echoed through the Elusian.

Fourteen

Evan

Tuesday 5:57 am
3 days, 16 hours, 52 minutes
until the falling

Pulling on my charred shirt, I crawled
through the hidden passage and limped
down the stairs.

I wondered if Henri would notice the difference in me. Would she sense the sapience? I pushed my shoulder against the heavy wooden door and limped into the entrance room. "Henri?"

The stool lay on its side. I pictured her sneaking through the shadows of the Elusian last night then shook the thought away. Voices came from a passage on the far side of the room. I followed them into a small hall that led to the pantries where Henri and I had been hiding yesterday. Muffled sounds came from behind a door Mazol always kept locked. I tried the handle. It turned.

Empty shelves lined the walls, except for a single chest. Henri sat on a chair in the center of the small room, staring at her toes, pale hands tight in her lap. Mazol and Yesler stood on either side. The door screeched on rusted hinges. Their heads jerked up. Mazol shoved me back into the hall. "You ain't allowed in here, gimp."

"She must have fallen asleep. Lash me instead."

Yesler pulled Henri out and threw her at me. Mazol locked the door with three different keys.

"We got more than lashes from her," Yesler said.

Mazol smacked Yesler on the ear. "Shut your hole." He pushed me into the wall. "Make sure you're both in the Caldroen in ten minutes."

"Henri can't work."

Yesler and Mazol crossed the entrance hall and disappeared down a passage.

"Hey!" I yelled.

Their footsteps disappeared as a door clicked shut.

I turned to Henri. "You alright?"

She didn't look at me.

"What did they do to you?" I reached for her hand.

She slipped it away. "I'm fine."

I watched her face. Sadness. Guilt. And more color in her cheeks.

"They let you off the stool early?" I brushed bread crumbs off her collar.

She pushed passed me. "We better go."

I limped to catch up. We walked silently. My stomach growled. I opened my mouth, last night about to pour from my lips, but I bit my tongue. We'd slept in the same bed for years, just two people keeping each other warm. How close can you be to someone and still not really know them?

She stared at the long hall, a tentacle stretching out in front of us.

I reached for her hand. "Henri?"

Our eyes met. A sad sort of twist stretched across her lips. A smile, I suppose.

"What was Mazol telling you when I came in?" I said.

Wrinkles formed on her forehead.

The monster whispered in my ear, filling that stale silence. *They gave her a meal to keep an eye on you.*

Then she turned and walked away, her feet padding the stone softer with each step until I heard only the warring of wind and windows.

Fifteen

Evan

Tuesday
6:23 am
3 days, 16 hours, 26 minutes
until the falling

I caught up to Henri five minutes past
sunrise.

Five minutes late.

We navigated the twisting, endless halls of Daemanhur on our way to the Caldroen. I limped along, a half-step behind her. The image of Little Saye hanging by her neck, her body tapping against the window, ran through my mind. And Anabelle's rash.

"Do you think Little Saye was sick?" I said.

"We're Roslings. We don't get sick."

"You're not supposed to die either."

"Little Saye... she did that."

"You really believe she killed herself?"

"What else could it be?"

"I've heard of sicknesses. Affliktions."

Henri went silent—her new favorite way of dealing with any question she didn't want to answer. Maybe it was just how she was dealing with Little Saye's death. I began to wonder what was possible with sapience. Could I break something? Put it back together? Heal sickness?

Anything you can imagine, the monster said.

But I had to resist sapience. I had to slow the countdown.

I suddenly stopped walking. "Do you hear that?"

Henri turned. "What?"

"Running, and"—I tilted my head—"breathing." I pointed down a murky hall. "That way." The footsteps grew. Henri stepped closer to me, gripped my hand.

"Hello?" My voice came back to me. At least, I think it did. I was about to ask Henri if she heard the echo, but the footsteps stopped.

"Evan?" Pearl appeared, silhouetted against the darkness. She ran to us, leaning over to catch her breath. "Anabelle... She's missing."

"It's past sunrise," Henri said. "Everyone's in the Caldroen."

"Anabelle woke up screaming last night. Then she was gone. I've been searching the castle for hours "

Henri looked at me. "Maybe she fell asleep somewhere. Lost track of time."

"Come with us," I said. "We'll check the Caldroen."

"I have to go." Pearl ran down the dusky hall.

We rounded a corner to a passage that ran alongside the Caldroen's curved interior wall. Four narrow, bronze-plated doors lined the right side of the hall, leading to furnaces that were used for cold-starting the Caldroen. The last door was ajar. Firelight flickered inside. I approached it slowly. The lock was busted. An iron pry bar lay on the floor.

I kicked the door open. "Is someone there?"

Heat blasted out. My skin grew sticky with sweat. I peered in. On the far side of the small room, the furnace door swung open. A body slumped against the threshold, lit in blue and red by the burning inferno.

"What is it?" Henri said.

I shook my head.

"Anabelle?" she said.

"I think she's dead."

"That's not possible."

Henri pushed past me. I held her back.

"We have to get her," she cried.

"I'll do it." I ducked in. The heat almost knocked me out. This is how crabs feel when they're dumped in boiling water. I grabbed Anabelle's arm. Henri appeared, helping me drag Anabelle from the room. I saw words carved into the brickwork by the furnace door.

Take it back

We pulled Anabelle's body into the passage. Henri slammed the iron door shut.

I leaned against the wall, my chest heaving. Henri, wrapping her arms around me, cried into my shoulder. Hot tears burned in the corners of my eyes, but they dried before rolling down my cheek. Those carved letters wouldn't leave me in peace.

Take it back.

Where had I heard those words before?

Take it back.

"Did you see them?" I said, "The words?"

"What words?"

"On the ground. It said, '*take it back.*'"

I spotted the star bracelet on Anabelle's wrist. Pulling away from Henri, I reached for it, and when the sooty metal touched my skin I was transported into a vision.

I made out a blurry shape standing next to my bed. It was Evan. He leaned over me. I kissed his cheek. Next to me, Pearl played with a wooden doll. Evan tucked us both in. I turned the little star bracelet over in my hand.

The vision faded—a memory from Anabelle's eyes, the moment I gave her the bracelet. The star had recorded her memory.

Henri reached for the rubric. "What is that?"

I shoved the bracelet into my pocket. "Nothing."

Her gaze lingered on me. I squirmed.

Mazol wants the rubrics. That's why she's curious.

Dravus said to keep the rubrics secret.

She's going to tell Mazol.

Despite the Caldroen's heat, I felt chilled. And suddenly, Henri's eyes didn't seem so red anymore. Had she really been crying, or pretending? But if I couldn't trust Henri, who could I?

The book said there was a man who would try to help me. Cevo.

Could Cevo keep me from turning into a monster?

I closed my eyes.

What's it like to be Cevo?

What's it like to be a master instead of a slave?

What's it like to have the power to save the ones you love?

Sixteen

Cevo

A rodent absconded from under my heel on its way to a hole in the groundwork.

Behind my back, I pinched my thumb to my forefinger. With a squeak, the rodent rolled onto his side, bursting into flames. I did not realize what I had done until the smell of burning rat reached my nose. Pretending to wipe my feet, I stomped it out, watching the Regents' eyes to ascertain their ignorance. Cevo, you must be more careful. Remember your vow. I swept ash under the table with my foot.

The Regents sat at a large oval table, staring at me. I glanced around, having not been in this room for nearly thirty years. Time had not been kind. A grand, round hall surrounded us with two wide staircases winding up the walls on either side and long gaudy curtains covering the windows. And above, a ridiculous chandelier that was likely as horribly out of style on the day it was installed as it is today. I stood in the Requestor's Booth, a chintzy, three-sided, waist-high enclosure at the foot of the table, where people from the city came to petition government officials. Do not lean on it Cevo; the whole booth might collapse.

"*Vice Regent* Mahalelel, is it now?" I smiled at him. Grandiose delusions for such a simple man.

Mahalelel glanced sideways at the elevated throne at the head of the table. "You didn't say the Chancellor would be absent from this special session of the Regency, Cevostramos."

I shrugged and wiped my feet on the rug.

He nasalized on, his mustache twitching like it always did when he was nervous, "Some people might get the wrong idea if they discover the Regency is meeting without the Chancellor."

I rubbed my white-gloved finger along the dusty edge of the Requestor's Booth. "Tell me Mahalelel, does this city have a cleaning staff?" From the dingy curtains to the tarnished brass hardware to the rampant mold below the windowsills, this place would better serve as a brothel than a judgment hall. A greenskin manservant brought a purple velvet stool for me.

I suppressed a shudder at the sight of it. "I am not so old I cannot stand." Imagine the bath I would have to take after sitting on that thing. I turned my attention to the fourteen olive-skinned men—like my adopted family. Humans born on this side of the mountains are not ebony skinned like me.

Cevo, you are an onyx sapphire walking atop a salt sea. This is why Mahalelel hates you, and he always will. The Regents stared with imbecilic eyes as I searched for just the right verbiage to pry my city back from their filth-crusted hands.

"Megestanis, let me get straight to the point," I said. "This city, obviously, needs money, and I am willing to provide it." I leaned over and picked up the table's dusty runner to illustrate my point.

"If you're finally willing to pay your share of the taxes," Mahalelel said, "you didn't need to waste our time by calling us here to say so."

Thirty years ago, I received a letter of absolvement from the previous Chancellor which indefinitely excluded me from my obligation to pay taxes on a city block that I had retained ownership of. I had, after all, been responsible for the entire city's existence in the first place — it seemed only fair to avoid paying taxes. But my role in founding El Qir had become mere legend to those at the table; humans have such short, pathetic memories. Especially when someone like Mahalelel is around, working day and night to make this city forget me. The terms of the Chancellor's tax absolvement letter had been disputed, but according to the agreement, the only one with the power to revoke it was the authoring Chancellor. And he happened, quite tragically, to die a few days after signing it.

Vice Regent Mahalelel stood up. "If you want to purchase one of the city's assets, you will find the bursar's office more than adequate."

"I'm afraid that will not do."

Mahalelel gestured to the Regents. "Good day gentleman. I have more pressing business to attend to."

I held up my hand to stop him. "I wish to purchase something a little out of the ordinary."

"Out with it then."

"The Chancellorship."

There was a moment of silence followed by an eruption of laughter. When Mahalelel seemed to realize I was serious, he coughed. "We already have a Chancellor. Quite popular with the people and only forty years old. We expect him to be Chancellor for some time."

And you would like to be Chancellor after him, would you not Mahalelel? Is that not why you want El Qir to forget me? "That is acceptable. I will wait."

"You'll wait?"

I looked behind me, pretending to search for the source of the echo. "Yes, I will wait."

The Regents shuffled in their chairs, trying with their limited mental facilities to figure out my angle.

"But the Chancellor has children," Mahalelel said. "The Regency chooses a successor only if there are no remaining heirs."

"Your terms are acceptable. Do we have an agreement then?"

"An agreement for what?"

"If the Chancellor should die while I am alive, and if none of the Chancellor's children are still living, I simply request this Regency to choose me as the successor. In advance."

"But the Chancellor has seven children. The odds are impossible that you would outlive them all."

"That is my problem, I believe."

I took a slip of papyrus from my lamb-skin satchel and handed it to Mahalelel. "My offer." His eyes grew large. A palpable buzz moved through the room as each Regent read my terms.

"You're a rich man to be sure Cevostramos, but —"

"I will have the money delivered tomorrow morning. Would you like it in gold or maladeum coin?"

"No one can afford to waste this much money on such a ridiculous gamble."

"I can."

"The people would never support the Regency selling the Chancellorship."

"Ahh, yes, that is the thing." I held up a single finger. "That is why you will all be sworn to silence. The purchase will be our secret."

"And all we have to do is promise to make you Chancellor if the existing Chancellor and all his children die?"

"Not a promise. A contract. I just happen to have it with me. Each of your signatures is all that is required. Just think, all the city's financial problems will be solved and you will have lost nothing."

I placed the paper, written in my own exquisite handwriting, outlining the details of our arrangement on the table.

"This says there are no circumstances under which the contract can be revoked?" Mahalelel said as he scanned the document, his mouth moving as he read. I remembered when he used to count on his fingers. Perhaps he still does.

"As you said, the odds are insurmountable that I will outlive the Chancellor and his seven children. Therefore you have no risk."

"Forgive me for being blunt, but what if they are...," he paused to clear his throat.

I raised my eyebrows. "Murdered?"

"We don't mean to be impolite," another Regent added. He didn't know Mahalelel as well as I do.

"Hmm... You do have a point." Several Regents murmured in agreement. I pretended to think, letting the hook sink in before speaking again. "*Vice Regent* Mahalelel"—I winked at him—"has an excellent point. Let us add a provision that states, 'As of today, if the Chancellor or any of his seven children are murdered, our agreement will be considered completely null and void.'" I handed the revised contract back to the Vice Chancellor.

Mahalelel stared at the contract like a Gylinn tax collector. "If there's no chance of Cevo getting the position through malfeasance, I don't see any reason to leave good coin on the table."

"We're nearly bankrupt," said another. "What choice do we have?"

One of them grabbed the papyrus. "Then sign the thing and be done with it." The others got in line. Mahalelel signed last, sealed it, and handed the contract back to me.

I smiled, but after a moment of reflection, my smile faded into disappointment.

Mahalelel turned his head slightly, as if he was trying to figure out what I was thinking. "You have your contract. We expect you to follow through with your end of the agreement, or we'll lock you up for failure to comply with an official ordinance. Gold coin will be sufficient. Easier for us to trade in." Mahalelel tidied up a few papers before him.

I put my hand on my heart. "I swear on the grave of my mother, it will be done." Mahalelel's eyes narrowed at me.

A door slammed open.

A rotund man ran in, huffing, his face red and soaked with sweat. "Regents!"

Chairs screeched on the brick groundwork as the city's leaders turned.

"I've just come from the..." The man leaned over, sucking in air.

"Breathe son," I said. "You are going to suffocate yourself."

"I have... very bad news..."

Mahalelel glanced at me with the eyes of a man who realizes he's just been checkmated.

The man took a long breath. "The chancellor and his seven sons are dead."

Seventeen

Evan

Wednesday
12:32 am
2 days, 22 hours, 17 minutes
until the falling

We slaved sixteen hours in the Caldroen
before Mazol let us go to bed.

Only eleven of us now: ten Roslings, one dark beast.

I lay awake next to Henri, tracing my fingers though her hair until she fell asleep. She hadn't been crying as much as the others. Trying to be strong. Her breathing steadied. I moved slowly, careful to not shake the bed as I sat up.

I sniffed the air. Smoke. Someone screamed. Henri's eyes snapped open. Firelight flickered under the door. Bursting into the hall, I stopped short. Flames rose from the rug outside our door. I grabbed it by the corner, beating it on the stone until the flames extinguished. Henri stomped out the last of the smoldering embers.

Another scream.

"Pearl." I dashed down the hall, ignoring the pain in my leg, and yanked open her door. Smoke billowed out. Pearl's bedsheets erupted in flames. Kicking, she rolled to the floor, taking the burning blankets with her. I pulled Pearl free as Henri beat out the blaze.

"What happened?" I said.

"The bed. I woke—it was burning."

"Did you see anyone?"

She shook her head, but her eyes kept finding their way back to me. Something in them made my stomach churn. Some secret accusation.

A thump against the wall. Pearl clutched the bottom of my shirt.

I pried her fingers free. "Stay here."

Henri followed me.

"Stay with Pearl," I said.

"I'm going with you."

Another thump.

I traced along the wall, trying not to make a noise. Reaching the door to the room next to Pearl's, I pushed it open, revealing a wall of clouded night. The room was filled with furniture, a maze of sheet-covered chairs and hutches and shelves and tables. In the dark, something crashed.

I stepped in, using my hands as a guide through the gloom. Henri held my shoulder as she followed.

Pearl appeared at the door.

"Go back to your room," I said.

"I don't want to be alone." She caught Henri's hand. I breathed in and moved further into the room. We made our way deeper into the maze. The glow from the hall grew dim.

Another crash. Wood screeched across brick.

"We're not going to hurt you," I said.

From the darkness, a whisper. "Take it back."

"Who's there?"

"Take it back!"

A tower of chairs fell on us. The room lit with red, flickering light. I scrambled to escape the tangle of furniture, pulling Henri free beside me. Smoke filled my lungs.

Coughing, I picked up Pearl.

"Get help," I said to Henri as I dropped Pearl into her arms. We turned to the door. Flames rose, licking the ceiling.

I saw a body. Lucy. Writhing on the floor in the midst of the flames. I lunged for her, but Henri held me back.

"I have to save her."

"The flames will kill you."

Henri ran to her instead, pulling Lucy from the sparks. Screaming in pain, she wrapped herself around Lucy, rolling until the flames extinguished.

"She's dying," Pearl said.

As Lucy shook on the floor, I leaned over, wiping her forehead, holding her hand. Then she went still. All around the room, flames went out in a puff of smoke. Her skin, covered in scratches and bruises and rash. Words, cut into her arm.

Take it back.

I turned Pearl away, hugging her tight.

Smoking embers littered the floor. Henri's face was sooty, her clothes charred. Pearl sobbed as I rocked her in my arms.

"We're all going to die," Pearl said.

"Shhhh. It will be alright."

"I don't want to die."

"I'm going to make sure you don't."

Henri flinched, like I'd just made a promise I couldn't keep.

Eighteen

Evan

Wednesday 9:12 pm
2 days, 1 hour, 37 minutes
until the falling

Twenty more hours slipped through my
fingers like wisps of smoke.

The countdown had not slowed, though I'd managed to avoid using sapience. I think. It's hard to know exactly what happens when you're asleep.

An hour ago, I woke outside Pearl's door to the sound of her crying. She'd discovered an itch on her neck. I wasn't any closer to finding out what was causing the Roslings to die. The affliktion—that's what I was calling it now. And I had only two more days before I would disappear forever. That is, if Mazol didn't figure out he's supposed to kill me first. I can only hope Terillium doesn't have another way to communicate with my uncle.

I massaged my temples, going through everything I could remember about the Roslings' deaths again and again. Combing for clues. Problem was, whole chunks of my memories were starting to fade. Twice in the last two days I'd woken somewhere else. One time I'd been unconscious for twenty minutes. The other time, three hours. A lot of hurt can happen in three hours.

I poured the sack of onyx iron rubrics into my hand. The star showed Anabelle's memories, but they were blurry. The vision only lasted a few moments. If one of these other rubrics worked like the star, only stronger, I might be able to discover the truth about the affliktion.

I put all the rubrics except for the skull back into the sack. Turning the door handle, I walked in. Pearl rolled over in her bed. When she saw me, I think she scooted away, if only just an inch.

"What is it?" she said.

"How do you feel?" I said.

"Just a little itchy." Her hands fidgeted. Her teeth chattered. She watched me inspect her. "I'm going to die, aren't I?"

"Everyone gets an itch now and again."

"Not Roslings."

I sat next to her. "I need your help." I lifted the chain from her neck and laced the skull on it. "Will you wear this pendant for me?"

She stared at it.

"I think it will help us find out what's causing the affliktion."

She dipped her head. The skull pulsed with shades of darkness when it touched her skin. The pendant seemed to draw any nearby rays of light to it. The sack of rubrics in my pocket vibrated. I heard a beating heart.

Pulling the little clanker from the sack, I felt rhythm beat through my body in time with Pearl's chest.

The sound of Pearl's heart beat inside the clanker.

Pearl grabbed the rubric. "It burns."

Radiance seeped out from her skin, like drops of blood, clinging to the skull before slipping inside through invisible pores. I ripped the rubric from Pearl's neck. At my touch, the globs of light reversed direction, penetrating into my skin.

I was transported into a vision.

I saw myself, but through Pearl's eyes, watching Pearl's memory from the moment the skull touched her.

The light stopped. The vision ended.

I put the rubric to my chest, felt a stab of pain. Tiny rays passed through my skin into the skull. The pain faded after a few moments. It was recording *my* thoughts now.

With some effort, I broke the skull's connection to my chest. I dangled the skull between us. If something happened to Pearl tonight, I'd be able to see it all when I retrieved the skull. I'd be able to see who was hurting the Roslings.

"Will you wear it for me?"

She eyed the trinket.

"It only hurts for a moment."

She nodded weakly.

"I'll be just outside if you need me." I kissed her check and went to the door.

She slipped the skull on as I clicked the door shut. Footsteps approached. I darted inside a room across the hall.

Henri appeared. She looked behind her then ducked inside Pearl's room. I moved to follow her, but my head felt suddenly airy.

No, not now. I can't blackout now.

I leaned against the wall for balance.

Stay awake, Evan. Stay—

My knees gave out. My vision expired.

Nineteen

Cevo

The Regents' mouths hung open as they
stared at the man who'd just told them
their Chancellor was dead.

I looked sideways at Mahalelel. He ground his teeth with an awful sort of scowl on his face. He wished he had thought of my plan first. He was always in my shadow. Always a few steps behind.

"Show me the bodies," I said to the message bearer.

"Who are you?"

"I am your new Chancellor."

I followed the messenger down a narrow, round passage and through the kitchens to a large nickel-plated door. Mahalelel and the other regents treaded along behind me like a herd of cattle who'd just seen a butcher's shop for the first time. The floor and edges of the door were covered in the rendered remains of hog carcass. How horrifying it would be if anyone important discovered I was chancellor of such a nasty, worthless corner of the world.

The messenger pulled the handle. Frozen air billowed out. I stepped inside, and my nose hairs instantly turned to ice. I pulled my barathea silk cloak around me as tightly as I could. The Regents folded their arms tight and huddled together as they followed. We walked past row upon row of hanging carcasses. There must have been more than forty, 200 pound hogs hanging by their hind legs, waiting to have their hair burned off before being sliced into bacon and ham and tenderloin. The dullgloom was bleak. I am not fond of inanimance, at least when the creatures are not stuffed by a proper taxidermist or cooked. Particularly not a whole pack of slaughtered pigs.

In the far corner of the icebox hung eight thinner shapes of various lengths. Like the pigs, they dangled upside-down by their feet. The shapes made me wonder: when men are frozen alive, do they die first or do they fall asleep before they die?

I turned the longest shape so its face could be seen. "Mahalelel, would you please identify this man for me?"

"You know well who it is."

"The Chancellor?"

"You murdered—"

I wagged my finger at him. "Whether they were murdered or not does not really matter at this point, does it? In the matter of the Chancellor and his sons, the agreement which the Regency just unanimously endorsed clearly states..." I unrolled the contract to read it verbatim. "'As of today, if the Chancellor or any of his seven children are murdered, our agreement will be considered completely null and void.' Everything that happened before 12:01am today is immaterial. I am, therefore, the Chancellor of El Qir."

I tried to ignore the shorter bodies hanging at the end of the row. I didn't like to see children mixed up in these kinds of affairs. Stooping, I pulled at the Chancellor's Lictor Ring, wiggling it back and forth on his frozen knuckle. I breathed on it a few times to warm it up and then placed it on my left thumb. The man's robes would be even more difficult to remove since he was completely stiff. I turned to the Regent standing nearest me. "Would you mind giving me a hand with this?"

He nodded dumbly.

"Better yet, you better pull them off for me." I stepped back as three Regents stripped the man, working the thick garment off one arm at a time. They helped me pull the stiff robes around my shoulders. I turned the old chancellor so his face was directed away from me, pushed past the gawking Regents, who I thought at that moment rather resembled hanging hogs, and made my way back into the kitchens. I passed a standing mirror and stopped to inspect my appearance. The brown color of the fabric was not flattering in the least, but the ring shimmered in a beam of sunlight. It looked as fine on my thumb as nearly any ring I had ever owned.

I caught Mahalelel staring at me. "I always thought gold looked delicious against my ebony skin."

He strode past me without looking again, passing into the judgment room along with the others. I took one last glance at myself in the mirror, watching over my shoulder at how the fabric swayed behind me, then followed the Regents in. I climbed the stairs to the raised throne. It, gratefully, was made of gold plated wood, not the reprehensible velvet on the rest of the Regents' chairs. The frosted Chancellor's robes draped heavy around my shoulders. And the Lictor Ring shimmered even more brightly now that we were out of the freezer. As soon as possible, I would have the fabric cleaned, but I was willing to endure wearing an expired man's dressings for a short while, if only to see the look on Mahalelel's face.

"Animus attentus," I said. "There is a matter we must attend to immediately."

The room exploded into commotion like the market streets of Carnis.

I held up my hands. "Silence!"

They obeyed.

Feeling rather embarrassed for losing my temper, I continued, "We are not getting off to a very good start, are we?" Adrenaline pumped through my veins. The hunt for Evan Burl was picking up speed. "When you woke this morning, you had no idea that today would be the day you are called to turn from your pathetic lives of self-indulgence and live a life of higher purpose. Allow me to reveal that purpose to you now."

Pulling something smooth from my pocket, I flipped it onto the table. It clicked across the surface, coming to a stop in front of Mahalelel. The Regents leaned forward, craning their necks to see.

An azul diamond.

"This city is situated on top of a mine, far below the city's streets, which I have been operating for some time. Thursday morning, the first day of Winterend Festival, my servants will break through to the surface —"

"If such a mine exists, it belongs to the city."

I frowned. "As your new Chancellor, I will steward it well."

"You've gone too far Cevo," Mahalelel said. "The people won't stand for this."

I stared at him, my fingers curling into a fist while I considered whether or not to send him into the dirt. A razor thin line cut across his throat. He fell off his chair, gurgling for air—

No, no. That is only in my head. Father would not approve. Mahalelel is still alive. I have to maintain control; I need him for my plan to work.

"You are not giving me enough credit," I said slowly. "I can be rather convincing, when I need to be."

"You're already the richest man in the city. Why bring this trouble upon yourself?"

I leaned forward. "The diamonds in that mine will help me find someone. If we do not find him soon, everything you love will be ripped away from you. You will stand as witnesses to the end of this world."

"Who?" Mahalelel said, "Who could be so dangerous?"

"His name is Evan Burl."

Twenty

Evan

Thursday
6:03 am
40 hours, 46 minutes
until the falling

"Why are your fingers bleeding?" Henri
said.

"They're fine."

I'd just stepped onto the landing outside the Elusian. Henri's face was inches from mine, our bodies pressed together at the top of the narrow stairs. Holding her torch higher, she peered over my shoulder into the closet. I latched the door behind me. Pushing past, I headed down the stairs. The blackout had lasted six hours this time.

"No, they're not fine." She tried to grab my hand.

I pulled away.

"Forget about it."

Henri clenched her jaw.

I pushed a door open and passed into a wide hall. "What were you doing in her room last night?"

"Whose room?"

"You know who."

"Were you spying on me?"

"No, I just..." The last thing I remember, Henri snuck past me into Pearl's room. I woke six hours later in the Elusian. "Maybe I imagined it."

"Wouldn't be the first time."

"What's that supposed to mean?"

"Just forget it," Henri said.

"We should check on Pearl." I pictured the faces of Anabelle and the other girls. My eyes burned. "Did you see her rash last night?"

Henri didn't respond.

I gripped her shoulder. "Henri."

"What?"

"Did you see Pearl's skin?"

She pulled away from me. "I didn't see anything."

"What if she has the affliktion?"

Henri walked on. "You think there's some kind of pattern, but there isn't."

"A Rosling has died every night since Sunday."

No response. I imagined gears turning inside her replacing flesh and blood. The thought of wasting the next twelve hours in the Caldroen made me want to punch a hole in the wall. I wondered what would happen if I didn't show up. If I told them I wasn't working ever again. Could Ballard make me work still, or was I stronger than even him? If I practiced sapience, no one could ever make me do anything again.

You could be great, a voice said.

No. I had to resist. I had to slow the falling. But sapience was starting to boil inside me and I was holding the valve shut on the kettle. The pressure pulsed in my blood, my muscles, my brain. The constant migraine and aching and pain caused hallucinations. I thought I saw Little Saye walking through the Elusian this morning. I called to her, but she disappeared.

Henri had gotten ahead of me. I caught up to her. The Caldroen grew near. My stomach twisted. Would we find Pearl's body in the Caldroen? I peered down a shadowed hallway. For a moment, I heard a set of footsteps walking along side us. I felt someone watching.

We turned a corner. The Caldroen's thick iron door lay open at the end of the hall. Six passages like this led into the Caldroen, one on each of the tower's six levels—ten-inch-thick cast-iron doors with spinning combination locks and twenty locking bolts jutted out from all four sides. Mazol said the doors were for keeping the castle secure from explosions in the furnace.

Henri entered first. Her glasses fogged up from the pungent air that roiled inside. She wiped the glasses clear. I stepped over the threshold. Hairs stood up on my arms. Walking to the edge of the third level mezzanine, I leaned out and scanned the room from top to bottom. Nothing. We made our way up three narrow spiral staircases to the top level, careful not to fall through the missing and broken floor grates.

At every turn, I expected to find Pearl, seizing on the ground or foaming at the mouth or still as a limp fish. I made my way to the brass finishing clanker. Limping slowly around the machine, I checked gauges, dials, and levers. Henri stuck the torch in a wall mount. Slumping into a window seat, she stared outside.

When I finished my inspection, I began the eight-step process of cold-starting the clanker. Why hadn't anyone else arrived? The sun would be up soon. I pushed a melanoid button and pumped a foot switch several times. Turning a dial so it pointed to the number fifty, I stomped the foot switch three more times. When I took my finger off the black rubber button, the clanker rattled then sprang to life. Wheels and belts and gears ground against each other. I pushed the dial to seventy. The clanker picked up speed.

The hot belt whirred—oil reserves must be low. I stared up at the long, silver lever high above my head that released more oil from the storage tank. It would be so easy to turn the lever with sapience. And I wanted to.

I glanced at Henri; she wasn't watching. Just one flick with my finger and the lever would point straight up. How I knew this was possible, I couldn't explain. I just knew. Of course, I could accidentally destroy the whole machine if my finger flicked too far. Or strangle Henri if my thumb twitched the wrong direction.

No one would know, a voice said.

The pressure boiled inside me.

It will be our little secret.

I clenched my fingers into a ball. Resist. You have to resist. I yanked a ladder from the wall, leaned it against the clanker. Wrenching the lever, it twisted off in my hand. A bead of oil dripped from the valve.

Hiding the lever behind me, I looked at Henri. She stared out the paned glass, arms wrapped around her knees. I breathed out. She twisted the dusky chain around her ankle, fumbled with the broken vialus base that hung from it. Rain streamed down the glass behind her. Somehow the rain always seemed to make Daemanhur feel even more huge and empty.

Over the rumble of my finisher, something clanked on the far side of the room. My eyes darted around the Caldroen. Nothing. Is paranoia a symptom of going crazy? Tension hung on the air like the smell of rotting meat. I moved toward Henri, sure something watched us from the mist. Henri smiled at me, the curve of her lips tinged with sadness. I saw a vision of gears turning inside her. Mazol stood at her control levers.

I opened my mouth to warn her of the danger I sensed, but stopped. Paranoia, I reminded myself, is surely a sign of insanity. And I was not going crazy. I was getting control. I was beating back the nightmare.

Laughter.

I smiled back at Henri. What a pair we made: a couple of pretenders. A strand of hair fell in front of her eyes. I wished I was close enough to brush it away.

A moment of silence filled the room. Beetles crawled under my skin.

Henri's sad smiled twisted with fear. "Evan, behind you!"

Icy fingers clasped around my ankle. Someone screamed. I fell face first to the platform, knocking the torchlight out of its mount. Darkness swallowed us.

A shadow flew over me. Something crushed my chest. I tried to flip over, but my hands were pinned. Breaking one free, I punched at the sunless mass above me but hit only air. I shoved my knee up. My attacker didn't budge. I reached for the broken lever, but it was inches out of my grasp.

Teeth sank into my shoulder. I yelled. Blood, warm and sticky, pooled beneath me. A glow flickered somewhere. I saw a dripping red mouth. And a mask. Yesler? Feet pounded up the spiral staircase behind us. My eyes blurred.

"Help him," Henri screamed.

Fists pounded my stomach. I curled in pain. "Take it back!" the man on top of me yelled. "I don't want it anymore. Take it back!" The voice sounded familiar, but thick and distorted. The shape was smaller than I thought possible from its weight. My attacker was about the same size as Yesler. Wore a mask like Yesler. But what was the source of his strength? Could he be a sapient?

Ballard appeared, ripping Yesler off of me. I struggled to maintain consciousness. Ballard yelled something. Yesler slipped free. I clasped my bleeding shoulder. One of my eyes swelled. Salty blood ran from my nose into my mouth. My head pounded as the room came back into focus.

A shadow flashed between two clankers twenty feet from where I lay.

"Over there." I pointed, coughing up blood.

The shadow darted past me. I saw his mask, different than any I'd seen Yesler wear before. I caught his arm, but he yanked away. Spinning, I fell on my face. I tried to get up, but my head still turned.

Yesler charged at Henri. She moved to the stairs. He jumped at her, arms transforming to talons. Cornered, she froze.

Rising to my elbow, I swung my free arm. I imagined striking Yesler in the side of the gut. Thirty feet away, the blow connected. Yesler's body flew sideways. An empty-sounding thud echoed through the Caldroen.

A dozen pairs of eyes stared at me. The Roslings had all arrived. I scanned their faces. Where was Pearl? I recognized their fear. Just like when jungle animals get too close to the gates. They were looking at a monster.

I rose to my feet, limped to the misshapen mass on the floor. Something about Yesler's eyes didn't look right. And he had covered his face with a cut of cloth.

Someone appeared at my side with a torch.

I glanced sideways.

Yesler stood beside me.

I turned to the body at my feet. I wanted to fall asleep. To dream. To wake up as someone else.

Sinking to my knees, I forced myself to pull the cloth from my attacker's face.

Pearl.

Twenty One

My body felt weightless.

This is how the dream always begins.

If I keep my eyes shut, can I stay here?

Can I make my father come for me?

Can I become someone else?

My eyes snapped open. Emptiness surrounded me.

Pure sky.

Stretching without blemish from one side of the big round earth to the other, the blue blanket was perfect but for a single dreary speck.

How can so much space feel so suffocating?

For what felt like hours, the whole world seemed frozen below me. Jagged, snow-capped mountains rose on my left. Endless jungles stretched toward the horizon on my right. And cutting across both, a bleached-leather belt of sand holding back the sparkling ocean. Somewhere, out on that big ocean, my father sailed. That's how I always imagined him. Sailing.

Except for a cool breeze, the world was silent. It seemed as if I could stay up there forever, like I was flying.

First, the mountains and hills lumbered toward me like big bullies begging for a fight.

Then houses and barns popped out of the ground, clumped together into towns and cities. And directly below me, a castle. My castle. Towers and walls, reaching out to me like hands from a grave.

Ten seconds later, what seemed like a bit of lint stuck to my eyelash transformed into a living human. Then more. Dozens, hundreds of servants. Working, eating, anything but looking up to see me swooping through the sky like a hawk.

Another ten seconds—far too soon—and the whole world rushed up at a speed that turned my stomach.

What happens after the falling?

Will I wake up as someone new?

I've never been able to watch all the way to the end. I tried to keep my eyes open, but right before I hit the ground I clenched them shut.

Twenty-Two

Claire

I woke up sweating; I'd been
dreaming again, always the same
dream.

Why couldn't I dream about gigantic chocolate cakes or swimming through a sea of custard or soaring with a flock of seahawks over a mountain made of baby blankets—flying is my absolute favorite. Why did I always have to be falling? I realized I was lying on a sofa outside my sister's room, but I couldn't remember how I'd gotten there. My sister, Ani, called it sleepwalking.

I couldn't remember anything before the dream, except...

Papa was coming home today!

Jumping up, I banged on the lavender double doors that led to Anastasia's bedchambers.

No answer.

I banged again, feeling smaller as I stared up at the towering doors. Everything in our house is so big, sometimes I feel like a miniature figurine hiding in a land of giants.

Sometimes I feel like I'm all alone.

"Let me sleep," Anastasia moaned—her voice muffled by doors and bedcovers.

I peeked into her room through a serving cupboard. "Cummon, Ani! Get up." I used to sneak into her room through that cupboard, but I was ten-years-old now—practically grown up—and Mother would have a fit if she caught me crawling around on my hands and knees. 'Not befitting of your station,' she would say.

"It's my birthday," Anastasia said into her pillow. "Leave me alone."

I fell into the chair. "If you don't get up soon, your birthday will be over." I kicked my feet against the wall, until a few moments later, the door lock clicked. Springing from the chair, I flew into the room as Anastasia stumbled back to her bed. My sister's room always smelled of peaches and vanilla. Papa shipped spices in from all over the world so we could make our rooms smell like sunshine or the sea or whatever we wished.

"The sun isn't even up yet," Ani said.

"It's been light for an hour." I ran to the windows, struggling to throw back the drapes. Mother says I'm too skinny. Ani says I'm too fat. When I can barely open the curtains, I tend to side with Mother.

Anastasia made a funny sound. I imagined a milk cow rolling under the covers, moaning from overfull udders. I giggled—then, pressing my face up to the window, gasped. "The ships!"

Ani jumped out of bed, elbowing me aside for the better view. "Papa!"

I shoved her back, pushing open the window. The smell of salty waves warmed by the sun-bathed walls of our home blew in — the breeze tickled my skin. Our house was nestled in the foothills of a great mountain range, high above the ocean. Three ships with bright sails and flags flapping rounded the cliffs floated into the harbor. I jumped up and down, screeching and waving, thankful mother wasn't there to scold us for 'acting beneath your station.'

Anastasia ran to her dressing room. Climbing into a window seat, I pinned my face to the glass. I watched the ships bob slowly into the harbor, catching my own reflection in the glass. My face didn't look as happy as I thought it should — I reminded myself of how Ani looks sometimes when she's angry, when she calls herself by another name. I remembered the fight my parents had before Papa left, something about having to go away for a long time. Maybe forever. Papa often traveled for weeks, even months at a time, but what if he was gone for years? What if he never came back?

I would be all grown up when I saw him again, if I ever did. Papa was the only one in the world who really understood me. I hated it when he was gone. I didn't think I could survive if he left for good. But maybe I would be happier if he *wasn't* coming home today, if I was never going to see him again. Might be easier than having to say goodbye forever.

A mouse crawled around inside me, twisting my insides, as I slid out of the window seat and tiptoed to the door. Before I could decide between running away or hiding, Anastasia burst out of the changing room. She caught me by the shirt. "Hurry, we're going to miss him."

Two handmaids with trays of hot pancakes, maple syrup, and spiced sausages walked up the stairs.

"Don't ye want yer breakfast?" Sophia said. "We was ordered t' bring it up early." From her accent, I guessed she was born in one of the poor towns of South Masr. She leaned close, her glasses pressing against Ani's ear, whispered without the accent, "We've been waiting a long time for this. Don't forget what I told you." I wasn't sure if she was talking to me or Anastasia.

"We should eat," I said, inspecting Sophia with squinted eyes. Around her ankle was a chain I'd never noticed before.

"But the ships are almost at dock." Ani stomped down the stairs, pulling me after her. We passed four more servants and turned three more corners. Rounding into the entrance hall, we skidded to a halt. Next to the three-tiered fountain bath in the center of the hall stood Duckie—and the giant mole on her nose—feet planted, arms folded tight. As far as I could tell, Duckie's job was to ensure Ani and I were dressed as uncomfortably as possible for whatever occasion presented itself.

I looked at Anastasia, then myself—white chemises and petticoats. Hundreds of people in town dressed less modestly, but they weren't Amadeuses. Our last name entitled us to 100,000 acres, a city of servants, and the finest armada on the seas. I'd trade it all for a swift ship and an endless horizon, but Mother said life didn't work like that.

The old woman straightened her portly body. The mole stared at me. "I 'spect you're not thinking on going out like that. Master Terillium won't like see'n his daughter look'n like a tuffin."

I sighed. "We better go put on a ruff and gown. Probably a hat too in this heat."

Anastasia raised her chin. "There's no time." She darted for the front door. I ran after her, and I swear, that mole followed me as I passed.

"Jus' a min'it, if you please!" Duckie caught Anastasia's arm, but my sister twisted free and pushed her backward. The old woman wobbled then fell into the fountain with a splash. I tried to go back for Duckie, but Ani pulled me out the front door and past a frowning, grumpy old man who had been the butler for as long as I could remember. We stepped onto the porcadia and into a bath of sunlight. In the distance, a dozen servants collected rose stems from the gardens that swooped down from our house.

"We should help Duckie," I said.

Ani slammed the door shut. "That's what servants are for."

"You didn't need to push her."

"She shouldn't have tried to stop us."

"It's her job."

Ani shook her head. "You're impossible."

"Just go without me." I sat on the wall of the fountain bath that filled the middle of our circular drive. The fountain's spray reminded me of playing behind waterfalls during summertime vacations to the mountains above our town.

She folded her arms. "Papa won't give us a present if you don't come."
Ani insisted that we do everything together. Sometimes I hated her for it.
I hesitated for a moment, wondering how much she'd hurt me if I refused
to come, then slipped off the wall and followed. As the horse barns came
into view, a stable boy—cutting off a yawn—jumped up to meet us.

"My horse," Anastasia said.

The boy's shoulders tensed. "Begging yer pardon m'lady, but
Stablemaster Braxton said you aren't t'ride alone."

Anastasia twisted his ear. "Don't question me pig. Besides, I won't be
riding alone, obviously." He bowed low then ran into the stables,
appearing a minute later with Anastasia's chestnut Connemara. Grinning
shyly at me, he tightened the saddle.

"Quit gawking at Claire and help me."

"I'm sorry m'lady. Here ye are miss—"

Anastasia pushed his hand away, yanked the pony's mane, and shoved
her foot into the stirrup. The pony moved and she slipped. The boy
caught her waist and lifted her into the saddle.

Anastasia whipped the boy across the face with the leather reins.
"Touch me again and I'll have you lashed in the square."

"I'm sorry m'lady, I—"

She looked at me. "Should I make him cut his own skin?"

I pulled myself up behind Anastasia, wondering if the small horse was
strong enough to carry two. "Oh shut up. He kept you from falling on
your fat butt."

"I'm so sorry m'lady. It won't happen again."

Anastasia kicked before I was ready and we jolted into a gallop.
"What's with the servants today?"

I barely stayed on. "Careful!"

"Don't be a ninny." Anastasia kicked the pony again and we surged
forward.

I wrapped my arms around her, trying not to think of the times she
made servants cut themselves, or hold their hands to a flame. She made
me call her by a different name sometimes. She talked about herself like
she was someone else. "Terisma wants to play." Or, "Terisma doesn't like
you very much Claire." Or, "Terisma will slit your throat while you sleep if
you ever tell on us." Last week she said, "You won't know it's coming.

One day you'll make Terisma so angry I won't be able to stop her. That will be the last night you go to sleep."

The wind swept through my hair; the Connemara ran as fast as if she was carrying just one. If anything could make me forget Terisma, horses could. To ride an animal so powerful and beautiful, sprinting across the ground like I weighed no more than a feather—as close as I could get to flying. I wondered if there were horses deep in the jungles that had wings, horses that could fly. I'm going to find one someday, when I'm grown up. I'll be a great explorer—like Papa.

I looked up at a flock of geese passing overhead. Lifting my arms from Anastasia's waist, I spread them in the wind. "If I could fly, I would carry you with me above the clouds, and we could go see Papa anytime we wanted."

"If you could fly," Anastasia said, over the clicking of hooves on the cobblestone beneath us, "I would dissect you like a frog and find out how you worked. Then I would learn to fly and you'd be dead."

I stuck out my tongue.

Anastasia's eyes narrowed. "If you're not nice to me, I might forget to stop Terisma from hurting you. The only reason you're still alive is I tell her to leave you alone." Clicking her mouth, she squeezed her legs to push the pony even faster. The great wall that kept us protected from the jungles outside our estate blurred by as the Connemara's hooves pounded the pavement like wood blocks in Bilielle's 3rd Symphony. Soon we were passing under the archway. Another ten minutes of galloping and we veered off the road down onto the hard sand, splashing into the surf. Crystal waves tinged with the scent of seaweed lapped up onto the hot white shore like a bubble bath, but as the city and docks came into view, the knot of worry in my stomach grew into a lump.

Didn't Papa want his family? Why would he leave us? But Papa had to love me. I could see it in his smile. My mind turned to the servant girl this morning.

"What was she talking about?" I said.

"Who?"

"Sophia, the servant. She said you've been waiting a long time for something."

Anastasia said nothing. After a minute of riding in the surf, we rejoined the stone road where many more people were also making their way to the wharf. We climbed several wide steps to the boardwalk, and the sound of the pony's hoofs changed from clacking on stone to the thud of worn timber. The crowds parted for us, bowing when they saw who we were. I saw dozens, maybe hundreds, of Papa's men about, readying for his arrival.

The largest of the three barques was nearly to the docks when we arrived. Written in large green letters on the starboard hull was the ship's name, *Elandian*. It was twice the size of the other two ships. If our mansion made me feel like a miniature figurine, Papa's ships made me feel like a flea. Men yelled back and forth as the crew on the ship threw ropes over the side to those waiting below. A dozen hands heaved on the ropes, guiding the ship the last few feet into the wharf.

The hull groaned as its shiny, perfectly cut timbers ground against the dock. Finally it stopped, bobbing gently up and down. I imagined *Elandian* was a wrinkled old woman like Duckie, but fabulously rich. *Elandian* even had a mole on her nose: a lantern hanging from the forepeak. Weary from a journey to the ends of the world and back, she was happy to finally be home.

A ramp clanked into place. Everyone stopped working all at once, like when the conductor taps his baton before a performance. At least a hundred servants and huge crowds of men, women, and children stood quietly, facing the ramp.

A white-bearded man stepped onto the plank, his skin wrinkled and tan. The uniformed workers remained silent, their arms stiff at their sides. But the crowd cheered for Papa, the great Lictor Terillium. I wondered what it would be like to have crowds of people cheering for me someday. I could be Lictora, Papa hadn't decided whether Ani or I would take over when he retired. He waved and smiled to the crowd.

We slipped off our pony and ran, nearly knocking him over. "Papa!"

With his arm around me, we walked the rest of the way down the ramp. I beamed so wide I felt my face might split in two. He seemed happy to see me, but I thought he looked tired—or sad—under the smiles.

The noise of dock-work filled the air again. Once the ship was properly put in, the crew would pour down the ramp and the whole town would be filled with happy families, just like mine. I imagined other families hugging each other... except they would know how long they had together, and I didn't have that. Sometimes I felt sorry for the sailors' families, but sailing was their job. They had to go away to earn money to feed their families. Papa didn't have to leave. He had enough money to last for a hundred forevers.

Townspeople bowed and cheered as we walked along the docks. Papa grinned down at me with a real I-love-you-more-than-anything smile. I squeezed him, as if to make sure that he was real. If Papa loved me that much, he could never leave forever.

Papa braced himself on a rail. "I've got something for you." He pulled both hands out of his pockets, his fists clenched shut.

We jumped up and down.

He gave a big eye-twinkling grin, the kind he saved for when he was truly happy. "Pick a hand." He unfolded long wrinkled fingers, revealing two bright silvery-brown bracelets covered with trinkets. Mine had miniature elephants and shiny gems that shone like stars and a vialus in the shape of an hourglass with smoke swirling inside and a flowering bonsai tree painted in colors I'd never seen. I focused on the elephants and for a moment thought I saw his feet moving. I imagined dust kicking around his legs as he crossed the desert on the west side of the mountains. One of the trinkets, an engraved oval locket, felt prickly and soft at the same time.

"Pretty!" Anastasia tried to grab the bracelet from Papa's hand.

"Hold a minute," Papa said, pulling the bracelets back. He lowered his voice. "These are made from malledeum. One coin is worth more than a whole chest of gold."

Anastasia tried to grab again. Papa held up a finger. "Patientiam, child. These little trinkets, they're called rubrics. Each has no equal. I've brought them halfway around the world just for my little lictora, even made a few modifications."

"What do they do?"

"They bring out your natural beauty, of course." He laughed, sliding them on our wrists. Then he whispered, "They also keep you safe." He stepped back and admired us. I shook the bracelet on my wrist. My skin tingled.

"No one can take these from you," Papa said. "They sting when other people try to touch them."

"I don't want to hurt anyone," I said. Papa smiled.

"Just enough to keep people from trying to take them. And when you touch them, you won't feel a thing." He beckoned to Anastasia. "See?"

She held out her finger, touched my bracelet, then jerked her hand back. "Oww." Anastasia gaped at her finger then put it in her mouth.

He laughed. "Just a little trick I learned in my travels." That's how he explained anything strange.

"Mine won't open." Anastasia's voice cracked as she pried at the side of the locket.

"Well, that's something else. They only work when you really need them." He winked at me. I felt a frown grow on my face. He could be giving us these bracelets to soften us up for the news that he was leaving forever. I had to ask him for the truth. He wouldn't lie, would he? Papa seemed to notice something was wrong. He opened his mouth, but someone interrupted him.

"She'll make a beautiful lictora someday, my Lictor."

I turned. An expensively dressed man stared at Anastasia as he strode toward us. Papa had so many workers it was hard to remember any of their names, but I think this man might have been the Mayor. It was like I was invisible to him. Didn't he know I might be lictora instead of Ani?

"Begging your pardon Lictor, but you have a visitor. He arrived just before you. Wanted to speak with you immediately after you came to land."

"I'll see him when I'm done with my girls," Papa said. "Oh, did the shipment from Yarrow Point come in while I was away?" Papa and the Mayor began to talk about business. Anastasia played with her bracelet, but I didn't want mine anymore, not if it was meant to make me feel better about Papa leaving forever. The Mayor talked on and on and I began to wonder if I would ever get a moment alone with Papa.

I wished the Mayor would just go away.

Sometimes I wondered if I could make things happen just by thinking about them. I asked Mother about it one time—the one and only time Mother has ever slapped my face. She apologized later, but told me to 'never talk about such foolish ideas again.' Papa just hushed me when I asked him. But I swear, sometimes I can do things that aren't normal. I tried to move a ball once, and it rolled away from me. Ani said I was just making stories up, but I wasn't. If I could, I'd make this man go away. I'd make him roll backward, like that ball —

The Mayor wobbled on his heels, waved his arms and fell backward off the dock. Papa's hand shot out, seized the Mayor by the shirt, and lifted him back to the dock.

The Mayor patted his chest and face as if checking to see if he was really there. "Thank you Lictor... I must have lost my balance."

Papa frowned in my direction. I thought he shook his head at me, a slight jerk of the neck that only I would notice. He turned back to the Mayor. "And here I thought I was struggling with my sea legs. Are you well?"

"Yes Lictor. I'm quite in one piece."

Papa's eyes settled on the man waiting for him. "Who did you say was here to see me?"

"He didn't give a name."

"I see." Papa stared at a man sitting on a bench at the far end of the docks. "Did he say whether he wanted to see my butler too?"

"No, Lictor. Shall I tell him you're unavailable?"

"I'll be with him in a moment."

Just go away! And then, just like snapping my fingers, the Mayor whisked off to the man waiting for Papa. I wished for the Mayor to leave and he did. Crouching next to me, Papa lifted my chin. "Sometimes I wonder about you."

"Are you leaving?"

"I'll be back before you can say babblebox."

I clung to him. "Babblebox."

"Why don't you stop by Santo's on the way home," he said. "Pick out a big tangerine-lime flavored lollipop and get an extra for me. I've been craving that man's sweets for six months." He handed Ani an iron drachma.

Anastasia glowered at the coin in her hand like it was a paulluse beetle. I imagined the beetle burrowing into her hand, then eating its way up her arm. That would teach her to be more thankful.

"We have a whole box of Santo's lollipops at home," Ani said.

"Hmmm," Papa said. "I see. Maybe you can sneak a peek at your present."

"Presents!" Anastasia tore off down the road toward Santo's.

Now I was finally alone with Papa.

He nudged me. "What's the matter with you."

"Oh, I..." My eyes fell to my toes. "I'm glad you're back." I hugged him, turned to go, then stopped. "I was just wondering..."

"Go ahead. You can ask me anything."

"Are-you-going-away-forever?"

His eyebrows furrowed. I silently begged him not to make me ask again. His face turned serious. A long terrible pause, the kind adults make sometimes before they tell you something horrible, like 'remember that nice little kitten we gave you? Well, it died. And we're not going to be getting another'.

"Yes," he said finally, "of course I'm going to have to go away again."

"I'm talking about forever."

"Forever?" He smiled, but there was no twinkle in his eyes. "Why would you think I was going to leave forever?"

"I heard you and Mother fighting about it months ago, before you left the last time."

"Ahh, well that would be why you're not supposed to eavesdrop. You might get the wrong idea."

He hadn't really answered the question. "Well are you? Leaving forever?"

"You remind me of your mother," he said. "Of course not. You're my little Bell. I could never leave you forever."

I watched him carefully. He didn't look like he was lying—there was a sadness in his eyes, but he was being honest. I touched his hand. "I love you, Papa."

"I love you too little Bell." He pulled off his coat and put it around my shoulders. "Wear it home for me, will you?"

Wearing Papa's old leather coat was my absolute favorite. Breathing it in, I smiled. Papa's clothes always smelled like tool oil and cedar shavings and the cologne Mother bought him each year for his birthday. I walked to the edge of the dock and onto the beach. Glancing over my shoulder, I saw Papa talking with the man who came to visit. The man seemed so familiar. They seemed to be arguing. Papa pointed at him and the man shoved Papa's finger away. I'd never seen anyone push Papa like that. I imagine most men would lose their hands for touching Papa in a way that didn't please him.

Shoving my hands into the coat, I walked slowly in the surf. Papa never explained how the worn old coat worked—it felt cool when the weather was hot and warm when the weather was cold. When I asked he said, "Child, you've got one healthy imagination," or "It's nothing. I picked it up from a street trader in the New Republic."

Playing with the pocket flaps, I felt the smooth leather. As I flipped the pockets open and closed, I saw a tiny zipper I'd never seen before. I slid the zipper and found a tiny leather book inside. It was mostly blank pages, a few with writing. A number of pages looked to have been torn out. What I read didn't make sense, until I came to:

Execute the boy immediately.

I read the note again. At the bottom I found a signature.

Terillium Amadeus

My body shook. I'd read stories about bad men who killed people, but now Papa was one of them. I imagined him signing his name at the bottom of the letter, grinning at the thought of a boy dying. Suddenly, I hated Papa for making me love him, for making me care whether he was leaving or staying.

I couldn't let him go through with it.

I had to stop him.

Twenty Three

Evan

Thursday
6:33 am
40 hours, 16 minutes
until the falling

I opened my eyes.

Pearl's skin was clawed and scratched; her fingers sticky and red. Blood covered her chin and lips.

My blood.

A vision flashed through my mind. Her teeth clenched into my shoulder; her mouth tearing flesh from bone. We'd always been so scared of what lived outside the courtyard gates. We should have been more worried about what lived inside.

My shirt weighed heavy on my shoulders. It, too, was soaked with blood.

A crash behind me. I jumped to my feet, caught Ravenna by the shirt. My other hand formed a fist.

Ravenna shielded her face. "S-s-sorry." I backed away. The noise came from a fallen rack of tools.

That's right, little girl, a voice said. *Don't upset the beast.*

My eyes drifted to Pearl. Ballard moved to lift her, but Pearl lurched. She pulled back into the shadow of a clanker, her gazed locked on me. A raw patch ran around Pearl's neck where the chain of the necklace lay.

She didn't blink. "Take it back."

Slowly she rose then lunged at me. Ballard grabbed her by the leg as she got her fingers around my wrist. Ballard ripped her away. She screamed. Spit flew from between her lips. He stuffed a rag in her mouth. Squirming and fighting, Pearl almost got away until all three Warts bound her feet and hands until she was no more than a rolled rug slung over Ballard's shoulder.

Mazol jerked his head toward the door. Pearl screamed into the gag, wriggling and fighting. I made out a single word as Ballard carried her out of sight.

"Murderer."

Pearl—the affliktion had taken her mind. She confused me for someone else. Mazol. Yesler. The real killer.

You gave her the skull.

"I was trying to help her."

You were trying to prove your innocence.

"No—"

I stopped. Everyone stared. They couldn't hear the monster—they thought I was talking to myself. They'd seen me use sapience. They'd seen me almost kill a ten-year-old girl.

"There's no way you could have known," Henri whispered.

"Known what?" I snapped.

"That it was Pearl who attacked you." She put her hand on me. I pulled away.

"What was that?" Henri said.

I avoided her eyes.

"What stopped Pearl from killing me?" she said.

I stared at a clanker behind Henri.

"That's why your fingers are bloody, isn't it? You've been using sapience."

I needed more time to figure out what was happening. I couldn't be causing the affliktion. Unless, the rubrics...

Pearl said, 'Take it back.'

'Murderer.'

Could the rubrics be causing the affliktion? No, Pearl started itching before I gave her the skull. I had to get that pendent from Pearl before Mazol discovered what it did. I moved to the door. Mazol stared at me. Yesler too. I expected anger, but their faces were stretched with terror.

After all those beatings, all those years of abuse, their fear was priceless. Yet dread wasn't enough. I wanted them to hurt. To feel my pain. I smiled. Fear made me smile. No. Because I could hurt them, I smiled. Revenge lay before me. All I had to do was reach out and take it.

And then I saw me as my father did. He was right about me. The heart of a nightmare beat inside me. I couldn't deny it any longer. I stepped back, pressed against a clanker. Still they stared at me.

This is your chance. Crucify Mazol. Save yourself.

I leaned over a rusted oil drum to support my sagging body. "I can't."

Then do it for the others.

I shook my head. Yet I watched my arm reach out toward Mazol. The monster was taking control. Images flashed through my mind.

A whirlwind circled inside the Elusian. The toys, the books, the pictures, all the things I'd so carefully collected, exploded before my eyes. The hutch crumpled in on itself. Debris whipped through the room, circling around me. The fireplace erupted with blue flames.

Nightmares or memories?

I'd been resisting sapience, hadn't I?

The blackouts. The waking up where I don't remember going. The forgotten hours. These were the moments when the shadow owned me.

Mazol and Yesler were frozen in place. My fingers clenched into a fist. Mazol clutched his chest. He'd be screaming soon—

Ballard burst through a door. The moment broke. I collapsed to the ground. He whispered in Mazol's ear. My uncle's mustache twitched, the kind of pleased tick I'd seen before. Some of the girls whispered to each other. Some stared. I couldn't leave them. I had to keep fighting. The images from the destroyed Elusian couldn't be real. It's not possible. No one can do those things. Not a sapient. Not a monster. Not me.

Mazol aimed a kick at Ravenna. "What're you staring at? Get to work!" He turned to Yesler. "Get the gimp—" He glanced at me, cleared his throat. "Get *Burl* bandaged. The others will have to make up for him until he's healed up."

Yesler didn't move.

Henri whispered into my ear, "I was right about you."

Mazol pushed Yesler at me. "What are you waiting for?"

"In the closet," Henri said, "I believed in you."

I shoved past Yesler, grabbed Mazol's arm. "What are you doing to the Roslings?"

Mazol pulled away. "I don't answer to you."

"Tell me the truth," Henri said. "Please."

I watched Mazol. He'd seen the letter before I stole it. He knew I'd turn dangerous someday. It couldn't be a coincidence that the Roslings started dying the same week I became a sapient. Mazol was the murderer. He must have been planning it, waiting until my transformation. He wanted everyone to think I'm the killer.

"Where's Pearl?" I demanded.

"Where do you think?"

"Tell me!"

"She's gone the way of a two week Shade."

The room spun. I grasped his shirt. "You killed her."

"We all saw what happened," Mazol said.

"I thought she was Yesler."

Roxhill and Othella started crying.

"Roslings don't just die," I said. "You did something to make her lose her mind."

"Why would I kill her?" Mazol said. "We can't run the clankers without Roslings."

Listen to your uncle.

I felt Yesler pulling me toward the door. Mazol flashed me a pearly smile. I lunged at him. Yesler tightened his grip on my arm. I ripped away. My leg brace caught on a clanker. The splint shattered. I felt nothing.

Sapience coursed through my blood. I lifted an oil drum above my head. Except, I wasn't touching it. The barrel floated. I stared up. How is this happening?

"No," Mazol yelled, "Don't do it!"

Something plunged into my neck.

My head split with pain. Yesler stood beside me. A syringe fell from his hand, empty but for a few drops of liquid coal. I staggered sideways. The oil drum crashed to the platform, rolled over the side, dropped six floors to the base of the Caldroen.

Someone whispered in my ear, "you're not who you think you are." The voice sounded like Henri's, but she stood twenty feet away.

Little Saye appeared. But Little Saye was dead. Wasn't she? Could Mazol have faked it? She said something I couldn't understand. Mazol grinned. Their voices rang in my ears long after the world melted, fading until just one remained.

You should have slaughtered him when you had the chance.

I didn't realize —

You better open your eyes.

But this isn't a dream. I'm awake.

Not all who dream are asleep.

How do I end it?

Slay the dream.

And what will I find on the other side?

That you're a monster.

...

I am a monster.

Vol. Two
Whispers

Twenty Four

Cevo

Children are like bovem dung.

While a necessary part of life, they are not something I am particularly fond of spending time with. I counted at least 121 of the little beasts in the crowd, cuddling their mothers, yawning, rubbing their eyes—I do not like to see the young mixed up in these kinds of affairs. The older children entertained themselves with mischief. Four threw rocks at boars. A cluster pretended to hang a smaller boy by his neck. A few others chased a limping cat with sticks.

As for the adults, tenacious and able-bodied, they filled the courtyard and streets as far as I could see. Thousands, shuffling about, whispering with mute anticipation. Yes, they suited my purposes well enough.

The inns of El Qir—the city I had raised from the mud nearly one hundred years ago—had been full for days; visitors slept in carts or pitched tents along the alleys. I would not have been surprised to find they lodged with bovems and dogs too. So much the better. I needed every hand I could muster.

In three days, the travelers expected to make a treacherous journey back to their homes—tree houses or thick-walled hamlets or castles buried deep in the jungles. The city would be cleaned; life inside El Qir's walls would return to normal. Or so the Winterend festival had gone for eighty-nine years. How will they react when they discover the gates are locked?

Vice Regent Mahalelel stood at the edge of the balcony.

"You do not seem happy to see me again," I said, leaning over the balcony rail beside him. He folded his arms and stepped off the dais. I cringed at the smell floating into my nostrils. My hatred for El Qir had increased in the thirty years since Mahalelel and I parted ways. This city used to be bonne bouche; the dock town to the east had been all but abandoned by migrants seeking their dreams in my shining gem. And now, my disgust was increasing in exponential proportion to the number of hours I endured these people's presence. I hated the way the alleys and streets stank eternally of horse and urine. I hated the manner of speech, pauper's vocabularies, and uneducated accents. I hated the way yesterday's meal stuck in their rotting teeth.

But most of all, I hated their laughter. Heads tilted back, wide putrid mouths, letting loose with rank, seedy joy. How I dreamed of knitting their mouths shut with silver threads. I could think of a thousand ways to end their laughter. I could invent a new punishment each day for a hundred years and never run out of ideas. I could make them cut out their own eyes, rip out their own teeth, shove their arms into a meat grinder. I am demiurgic like that.

—and yet, I had my vow.

29 years, 324 days since the last time I broke it. Mahalelel would remember that well. I wasn't about to end a record streak like that on the slack-jawed, sewer-dwelling rats who stared up at me. With trembling fingers, I produced a worn scrap of paper from my cloak's inner pocket, holding it close so Mahalelel wouldn't see. I read the words again, seeking the strength to maintain control.

Voveo.

I devote myself to cleansing the world of sapience and all those who practice it.

I abnegate forever sapience, and all its derivatives, unless such use is required to fulfill this vow.

Finis.

Cevostramos Tervereous Magmilliano

A simple vow; a contract of chastity. The difficulty comes in execution. I will not rip these heathens' tongues from their mouths. I will not bleed their eyes. I will not twist their lungs and intestines into a knot. Bend them to your will, Cevo, just abstain from sapience.

I wiped the balcony rail with a piece of cloth before placing my bleached white alligator-skin gloved hands on it. The hammered-thin gauntlets cost more than the citizens of El Qir earned in a year, but fine embellishments like this are worth every bronze coin, especially in the uncivilized regions of the world.

The sun hung in the sky midway to its peak, climbing tirelessly as it had the last 500,000 days we had spent ruling this earth together—yet the sun got all the glory while I got my hands dirty. Condensation clung to the grass in the shadowed courtyard.

Scaffolding rose around the lamp post in the middle of the courtyard; two gagged and nearly naked humans faced me across the empty space between us. Stretched in four directions, their arms and feet were tied to ropes that ran through pulleys to a team of horses. Everyone loves an execution, yet a tension lay across the courtyard—like having a guest show up to a dinner party naked. No one wanted to stare, but no one could keep from looking either.

Two rag dolls were pinned to my balcony, representing the two humans, or juras as they were called during the festival. The festival began when the Chancellor, I, poured wine on one of the dolls, condemning one jura to death. The other human received forgiveness and was celebrated as the Winterend Honorarius.

My armored guards begirded the crowds in the distance, a chinkless ring around the courtyard, glistening like a silver noose. I leaned out, waved to the people. "People of El Qir." I imagined women from the crowd confessing adoration for my baritone timber—not an uncommon occurrence. "It is an honor to serve as your new chancellor during Winterend." Small lies like this are necessary sometimes; do not feel guilty Cevo. "It is with love that we remember our great leader who passed, but I believe he would have us enjoy this festival and not mourn our loss." The people need a leader who understands their pain. "The festival is almost upon us. Bring me the wine of the jura."

The crowd cheered—that is good—thinking about jura blood instead of the guards forming ranks at their backs. My arms spread wide—the sort of thing crowds like—as the festival undersecretary brought me the most beloved city relic, the Winterend Goblet, filled with red wine. I caught my reflection in the gold cup—speckled skin, white mustache, short curly hair catching the lustrous morning; who would not want to see that face staring back at them every day?

Smile Cevo. The people's eyes are upon you. The crowd chanted, "Hagnus," the name of the one they wanted released.

I beckoned to Mahalelel. "Who is she?"

He didn't answer. I turned, raising an eyebrow at him.

He coughed. "A jungle traveler, she has no family."

"A hardy woman to be sure." I regarded her more carefully. "Or, girl, I think? She cannot be more than one and twenty."

"She took up residence three weeks ago with the poor of El Qir," he continued, "living in the city's walls. She has been requesting your audience since the day she arrived."

"Why didn't you tell me?"

"Would you have seen her?"

I paused. "I see your point."

"Hag-nus, Hag-nus, Hag-nus," the crowd chanted.

"What is the man's crime?"

"Odegaard, landlord of twenty-four units in Bitter Lake, accused of pyromancy. He burned three houses to the ground because the tenants refused to pay their rents. He locked the families inside before setting the fires."

I dabbed my lips with a cloth. "And the woman?"

"Hagnus stole a single loaf of bread from Roanoke Baker in the lower village. The people say she's ill for luck, becoming jura for something so small, a mere loaf of bread. And she stole the bread just this morning."

Juras are chosen by the last two crimes committed in the city, no matter how diminutive. I do not believe in luck. Priding myself on efficiency, I followed the letter of the law. Laws are beneficial for controlling the masses.

"I would rather not sacrifice either of the juras," I said.

"It's your law."

"That was seventy-six years ago. I think so differently..." Now that I have mines to run. "Have you considered slavery?"

"For what?"

"As a replacement for execution. Capital punishment is like slaughtering a perfectly good draft horse." Plus, every time I blotted out someone's life, I created a whole lot of work for myself. I had to hunt down every last brother and daughter and second cousin and assassinate, or adequately maim, every one of them in order to ensure myself a peaceful life, or at least a life that did not require constantly looking over my shoulder. For whatever reason, humans are often more understanding of enslavement. Plus, you get the added benefits of free labor for a decade or so, however long it takes for the slaves to die.

"The people came to see a killing," Mahalelel said.

I sighed. "You are right, I suppose." If they didn't get one, they might revolt. This would result in additional loss of labor, and perhaps, if my guards could not keep them in line, I would be forced to break my vow.

"Hag-nus, Hag-nus, Hag-nus." The people stomped and clapped and laughed. How can anyone think with such rank seedy joy running rampant in the streets? Give the people what they want Cevo. Slay the male jura. Free Hagnus—she was so young after all. Practically a child, and I do not like to see children caught up in these messy affairs. I held the goblet over the dolls.

"Hag-nus, Hag-nus, Hag-nus!"

I started to tip the wine over the male doll, but stopped. Something about this did not sit right in my stomach. Should I really kill the man?

"What are you waiting for?" Mahalelel said.

"Quiet!"

But he was right. Why should I care? These two juras were less than mus stercus to me. I am Chancellor. I am more powerful than the sun. I am one of the Three. I am Cevostramos.

Tipping the glass a little more, a bead of wine pooled at the lip of the cup. I stared at Hagnus. She glowered back with unblinking twilight eyes. Though she was gagged, I detected a hint of smile on her lips, like we shared some wicked secret. Perhaps she was merely confident in the crowd taking her side. Or something else?

Her features struck me as familiar. The crowd grew restless. They wondered why I hesitated. A fair question.

But why did Hagnus become jura? No one committed petty crimes this time of year for fear of being strung up for Winterend. Yet this woman got caught stealing bread hours after I became Chancellor. She must have *wanted* to become jura.

The crowd booed and slapped their hands. A warning. The last time anyone threatened me like this I broke my vow, and I mean really broke it good. Mahalelel was the only one who lived, and only because my father wouldn't have approved of slaughtering him. But why should I care if Hagnus wanted to be jura? I did not need a riot, not now that I was so close to finding Evan Burl. I stared at her eyes as I tipped my glass on the male jura's doll.

Then I saw it.

I jerked the glass back, sloshing wine on my white coat.

How shortsighted I had been not to put it together sooner. She did become jura to get my attention, desperate I would notice her. A pattern I have seen before.

Usually women like Hagnus hide from me. My vow compelled me to hunt them down. I found pleasure in coming upon them secretly, wrapping invisible fingers around their necks while they slept. But sometimes, the especially foolish ones came looking for help. Hagnus must have heard stories. She thought I could make her understand what was happening to her, maybe cure her. Maybe help her grow stronger.

I filled my lungs with air. Surely if she had been closer, I would have noticed sooner. Yet even at this distance, I sensed her power. I drew her scent into my pores. The hairs on my arm stood on end. Positively electric.

Little Hagnus was not as harmless as she seemed.

Little Hagnus was a sapient.

Someone shouted, "Let her go!"

"This ain't right."

I should just lynch the man now, deal quietly with Hagnus later. That is what Father would do—

"If you won't do it," Mahalelel said, "I will." He grabbed at the goblet. Wine sloshed on my hand.

I shoved him back. "You forget your place, little brother."

"You are no brother of mine."

"You are correct, *adopted*-brother."

"Father would weep if he saw what you've become."

"Enough!" My eyes darted from Mahalelel to the people in the streets. I thought I would see fear there, written on their faces. But I saw only contempt. The people had forgotten to fear me. Mahalelel had forgotten to fear me.

Mahalelel stepped close to me. "I used to be jealous of you, that Father kept me in the dark. That he taught you sapience. And you, you aren't even his real son. You're just an orphan."

"Silence fool."

"I realize now why Father spared me. He kept me from sapience because he loved me more than you."

I lifted my hand to strike him down, but someone from the crowd shouted. "Murderer!"

Others joined. They began to chant. "Murderer! Murderer! Murderer!"

Only when necessary.

I crushed the 300 year old Winterend goblet in one hand, wine burst between my clenched fingers, dripping to the dusty street below like egg mixed with blood.

Peace. Mouths hung slack. I shut my eyes for one euphoric moment to drink in the sound, then, ripping the bottle from the undersecretary's hands, I threw it at the scaffolding above both juras. Wine splattered across their faces. "Tear them both to pieces."

Then I stared down, daring them to give me one single reason to break my vow.

Twenty Five

Evan

Thursday
9:29 am
37 hours, 20 minutes
until the falling

Someone rubbed my arm.

I tried to focus and saw Yesler and Ballard standing over me. My head ached; someone might have been pushing needles through my skull.

"You're doing it wrong," Ballard said.

"What would a worthless lump like you know about it?"

"You're supposed to gauze the wound then use a pad that won't stick to it before putting on the wrapping."

I tried to lift my head. Some kind of haze swallowed me; I felt smothered, chained to the bottom of a lake. Images and sounds broke inside my head; nightmares from the restless spell I had been under. Pushing the images away, I tried to focus my strength, to find the power to fight Ballard and Yesler off. I had to find Pearl. But my body wouldn't cooperate.

The floor appeared in blurry detail. A scorpion seemed to stare at me, about six inches from my face. It took a few steps, paused, then scurried off.

A shadow appeared. Blurry, then sharp. The head of an asp leaned over me. It swooped down, fangs dripping with venom. I covered my face, but it didn't strike. When I looked again, the asp was gone. In its place stood Ballard. He rubbed gauze on my arm.

"Pity we have to clean it at all," Yesler said. "We could save time and take off the whole arm." Yesler lifted my head then poured something that tasted like vomit mixed with oil into my mouth. I sputtered. He held my mouth shut until I swallowed. The world tilted sideways. Their voices grew faint.

Flexing my stomach, I tried to sit, but gravity wouldn't release me. Nightmares floated up through the cracks in the marble landing—corpses' hands pulling me down into the earth. Creatures appeared. Faces. Little Saye. Anabelle. Lucy. They said, "time to sleep."

"You should be more careful," Ballard said.

"Why's that?"

"He could get angry."

"I'm not afraid of Mazol."

"Not Mazol." He pointed at me, only the tip of his finger in focus. "Him."

"The gimp's an eggplant." Yesler kicked me in the gut. "See."

"He won't sleep forever."

"He's always sleeping. Even when his eyes are open."

Footsteps moved down the hall, their voices grew faint.

"Evan didn't do anything to deserve this," Ballard said.

"He was born. That was enough."

"Maybe he'd turn out different if he had a proper family."

"You want to be the gimp's daddy?"

"No—"

"None of us have fathers; we turned out fine."

"I had a father."

"Yeah, and he beat you stupid..." Yesler's voice faded.

I tried to keep breathing, pushing my hands against the floor. Had to fight the dreams, had to find Pearl, but the hands were vices. They pulled me through the marble floor, into the nightmares, into a gravebox buried beneath the tiles.

Pearl lay next to me. She stared, eyes white. Her lips never moved, but she spoke. "You said you'd take care of me."

"The skull—" I started to say.

"I don't want it anymore. Take it back."

Then, right before I blacked out, I thought I heard the sounds of a party.

Twenty Five

Claire

Everyone over the age of thirty must think kids don't grow ears until they start shaving.

I've heard adults talking about how spoiled I am plenty of times, and they're probably right. But I'm tired of being one of Terillium's spoiled daughters. I don't want any more furnished dollhouses or Connemara ponies or pink silk dresses with curled ribbons and bows or diamond stud earrings or whipped banana pies. I saw a picture in Papa's office one time, an elephant with ears so big he could fly. Maybe my ears are too small; maybe they'll grow so large that by the time anyone notices I have them, I can just fly away.

But I can't fly away, not yet at least. Until then, I guess I have to put up with Miss 1000-Times-More-Spoiled-Than-Me-Anastasia and her birthday party, pretending the smiling man with the skewer behind the cake isn't a murderer.

By nightfall, hundreds of servants had transformed our courtyard into the kind of birthday fantasy world that made regular old spoiling look like a night in the stocks. Cakes and cookies and treats hid around every corner; I didn't eat a single one. Pink and white lace draped from every balcony, but I thought they looked like the ones Papa used last year. Countless candles hung in overlapping rows filling the courtyards and gardens with flickering sparks; irresponsibly dangerous. Then there were the fire breathers and musicians and jugglers and story tellers and fat little women in scary masks and skinny tall women in scary masks and unicyclists and clowns and men on stilts surrounding me for as far as I could see in any direction. Boring.

All through the night, guests presented Anastasia with birthday gifts (you would think she was already Lictora with the way these people were acting) and, as was tradition, gave me matching presents. Papa insisted his daughters be spoiled equally. A dozen handmaids were standing by to whisk the gifts back to our rooms when we were done playing. I made up a story about not feeling well so I didn't have to open any of them. I didn't want to make the guests feel bad—it isn't their fault Papa's a murderer.

The party stretched on forever. I just wanted to go to bed. Papa filled the air with tiny floating sparkly lights that tasted like vanilla or banana or mango or chocolate if you caught one in your mouth—not that I tried to. Then there were the dancing ballerina dolls in the fountains. They twirled and spun, gliding out across the water's surface and no one could explain how. 'Just something I picked up in my travels.' And no party is complete without floating fire-lanterns.

At 9:00, as the bells that hung from our home's tallest tower rang, the dancing ballerinas paused their pirouettes. The candles and torches and floating lights dimmed, until the whole courtyard grew dusky as the jungle's under-canopy outside the city walls. The stars seemed bright as flames, until they too, seemed to dim, like layers of fog had rolled over us. It became so dark I couldn't even see my own hands in front of my face.

Folding my arms, I leaned against a lamp post. I had a headache and had seen the whole routine before. Everyone went silent as little flames appeared deep in the fountain bath. Though the water was only a few feet deep, it appeared as if the orbs were further away than the stars in the sky. Slowly, the flames grew brighter and brighter until the first fire-lantern broke the surface of the water, sending soft circular waves out like raindrops in a puddle.

Everyone gasped.

The fire-lantern, shaped like a ship, didn't stop. It emerged from the water, dry and burning bright. It took flight and sailed up into the sky above us. Why couldn't I have been born a firelamp?

Soon, a second, then a third and fourth fire-lantern joined the first until the sky was filled with warm flickering flames. That, however, was not why everyone watched with held breath. They were still waiting for the finale. With a fizzing crackle, the first floating lamp imploded, as if it had been swallowed by the night. Then it burst with a gut shaking boom into a canopy of shimmering sparks that fell around the entire party.

Everyone cheered at the sight. I plugged my ears. One by one, each fire-lantern followed the first. They began to explode faster and faster until the sky was filled with every color. Shapes of flowers and ships and scary creatures of the jungle devoured one another, falling like a fountain around us. The umbrella of radiance shone so bright it could have been noon on a summer day.

Then, right before the end, all of the ashes and sparks which had long since fallen to earth, shot up together as rays of white into the starless sky until the fire-lanterns themselves seemed to become shimmering stars. The party-goers seemed to be sucking up every last moment as if it might be the last night they had to live.

I busied myself making sure all my finger nails were exactly the same length. Finally, after what felt like hours, everyone roused from the trancelike state they had fallen into. The musicians struck up a tune. The ballerinas danced. And the party entered its second half. This night was never going to end.

Anastasia made me come with her—like always—quietly threatening Terisma on me while I slept. I followed as she danced in the courtyard, played in the garden mazes and under the stilts of the high-walkers, laughed at the clowns, and tried to distract the musicians from their sonatas—violin and bell melodies that sounded ghostly after what I learned about my Papa that morning.

During the party, the house was off limits to anyone but a few servants, so Ani and I could have a place to rest. It was nearly time for cake when Anastasia decided she needed a break. She wanted to try on a new dress that shimmered like it was lit with flames.

Inside the house, the guests' noise was muffled behind the thick stone walls. Papa offered to give us both rides up to my sister's changing room. I refused, choosing to walk slowly up the stairs while he ran past me with giggling Ani on his back. I thought they resembled an ostrich with a fat pig riding on its back.

After he was done with Ani, I darted behind a bookshelf and snuck to the edge of the balcony just as my mother walked in. The entrance room was round, at least as tall as it was broad, with a white paneled, arch ceiling. Duckie called the style bar-oak, or something like that. It looked gaudy. Bright oil lamps lined the walls and one oiled-bronze chandelier, with hundreds of little flames, hung from the center of the arch above where I crouched. The servants set the lights to burn low at this time of night, so the room was dim and eerie. The marble floors, which helped keep the house cool in the summer, were covered with elaborately embroidered tapestries that Papa brought back with him from trips over seas. Two wide staircases made from paneled wood and platinum embedded stone curved up each side of the round room and met in the center, where I hid.

Not ten feet from me, standing next to a small hutch along the wall, I could see my mother frowning at Papa. "Is that behavior really appropriate for someone of your stature? And at your age? You could kill yourself."

"Ha. Imagine that?"

She didn't smile.

"I was just having some fun with my daughter," he replied. "You should try it sometime."

"You have enough fun for all three of us."

"Sorry." Papa held his arms up like a surrendering soldier. "Let's not argue about that again tonight, alright?"

He put his hand on her shoulder. She pulled away.

"What do you want from me?" Papa asked. "You have everything you've ever wanted. You live in the finest mansion for a thousand miles, your pantries are stuffed with the best food and wine, and you have a beautiful, healthy family. I return from months at sea, and you act like you didn't even miss—"

"If I wanted a fool to entertain me with platitudes, I certainly wouldn't have married one. You know why I'm upset."

Papa paused, shifting his weight from one foot to the other.

"I haven't decided yet..." he said.

Mother folded her arms under her breasts, making it look as if her dress's neckline was cut too low. "We can't keep living like this. You promised you would decide by the time you returned."

"It's not as simple as you think."

"Everyone is going to figure out that something is wrong eventually," Mother said.

"I'm careful," he said without looking at her. "They won't figure it out."

"You're still giving your daughter rides up the stairs. If anyone did the math, they'd have to assume you're at least ninety years old. What are you going to do when they start asking questions?"

"You sound like the man who came to visit me today." Papa pulled a blade he often carried from his belt and placed it on the table. I had seen the knife before; Papa always got a gleam in his eye when he stared at it, like it was even more beautiful than Mother.

"I heard about him," Mother said as she eyed the blade. I wondered if she was jealous. "I don't like that man."

"No one does."

"What did he want?"

"He never changes. Thinks I should give it all up. Just like you."

Mother's eyes shot up at Papa as he polished the blade on his sleeve.

"I'm trying," he said, "but it's not as simple as you think."

Sighing, Mother leaned her back to the wall. Maybe if she didn't insist on women wearing those insufferable corsets, she could breathe easier.

"I'll never know why you don't get along with him better," Papa said. "You two agree on so much."

"I won't let you hurt this family just to protect your secrets. I'd rather you say good bye to us and leave, than leaving me to explain what's happened to you someday when you disappear on us."

I crept forward.

"You know I won't do that."

"The day will come eventually, and when it does I'll be left with the mess."

Papa tested the blade's edge and drew a drop of blood from his thumb. I gasped out loud then clamped my hands over my mouth to keep from making any more noise.

"Would you stop playing with that thing," Mother said. "Someone's going to get hurt." Papa made a look that seemed to say 'that's the point.' I'd never seen Papa bleed before, not even one time when he was bitten by a huge Doberman. Not even when a criminal tried to murder him with a fountain pen in the courthouse. The Bloodless, that's what the boys in town called him when they thought no one was listening; Anastasia said she heard Papa's veins were filled with the stuff stars were made of.

"I wonder what you're hiding from me sometimes," Mother said. "Can't you trust me with the truth?"

Papa opened his mouth, but stopped.

"You used to love me... or was that a lie too?"

"Of course not. I still love you —"

"Then fix this."

"I've done everything I can." Papa stabbed the blade into the table. "You think the stone walls I built around this mansion are just to keep the cannibals out?"

"I don't care about a fence."

"You're protected here."

Mother's eyes narrowed and she spoke quietly. "From secrets?"

"No one cares about hiding the truth more than I do."

"I'm not sure anymore," Mother said. "I know you can hear the people whispering. Sometimes, I actually think you like it. You want them to know."

She turned and walked to the door, but Papa reached out and clutched her hand.

"You're right. It's hard for me..." He paused. "But, I made a decision while I was away. I took measures to ensure my family will be secure forever. I'm close to giving it up; I just need a little more time."

What measures? Killing Evan Burl? Is that what would keep us safe?

"And in the meantime?"

"I gave Claire something today. She's as protected as she can be."

She walked to the door. "It's time for the cake. Are you sure it's big enough?"

I startled at the sound of the door slamming shut. Mother didn't even ask. She didn't care that Papa had ordered a boy's execution. Papa lifted the pea coat from the chair where I'd draped it that afternoon. Slipping the coat on, he pulled out a bundle of loose pages from the desk drawer. He flipped through them, stopped to lick his finger, then turned one more. He sucked in a short breath. I watched his eyes dart across the same page three times. He slumped against the wall, sighed, then stared across the room. The clock behind me ticked off two whole minutes before Papa moved. I was beginning to think he might have fallen asleep when he stood suddenly. He felt in each pocket of his coat, one by one. I realized

I'd forgotten to put the book I'd stolen back. I scanned behind me, trying to think of where I could run.

"Claire!" Papa yelled.

I heard his boots pounding up the stairs. Stuffed in my stocking, the book felt hot against my skin.

"Where are you, Claire?"

Pushing my shoulders back, I stood up straight.

"Yes Father?" I tried to use the expression my Mother wore whenever she argued with him.

His eyebrows furrowed. "Have you been hiding up here?"

"Yes." I took a step back.

"And you heard what your mother and I spoke about?"

"Yes," I said, tilting my chin up, resolved not to show my fear.

"Tell me the truth. Did you find a little brown book in my jacket?"

An itch grew where the book touched my skin.

"I won't be angry if you tell me the truth now," he said. "I just need that book."

No turning back now. "I don't know what you're talking about."

His bright eyes flicked back and forth, like he could read my deepest secrets by staring straight through my skull, but I was determined not to look away.

"Come here child," he said, beckoning to me as he sat on a chair at the top of the stairs. I obeyed, trying not to shake.

"When I was young like you, figuring right from wrong was simple. But as I grew older, I realized some people seem good when in reality they are not." He placed a hand on my knee, as if to comfort me, but might it be to keep me from running away? "And some scary people are actually good. When you are a child, it can be hard to sort the scary people from the good ones."

Papa's other hand was behind his back. I pictured the dagger. Was he holding it now, ready to slit my throat if he discovered what I knew? I wanted to call for Mother or Ani or the servants, but he could smother me before the words left my mouth. I swallowed. "Which kind are you?"

"Neither." He furrowed his forehead. "I need you to trust me."

I took a breath. "Yes, Papa."

"That's good. But there's one more thing." He glanced in the direction of my ankle, where the book was hidden. "If you happen to find that book, and if I'm no longer able to carry out what it commands, will you promise to see it done?"

I imagined him tightening his grip on the sable knife. If I didn't agree, he would kill me.

"I'm trusting you to be Lictora one day. That day may come sooner than any of us expect. I have to believe you'll do what needs to be done."

I pictured him slumped against the wall and reading those loose pages. What did he read that upset him so much? And why was he talking suddenly about me being Lictora sooner than we expect?

"That's good." He patted my head and I thought I saw him slip the blade in his belt. "Black and white worlds are the luxury of children. I'm sorry to be the one to tell you so, but better to learn from your Papa. Life's a much crueler teacher."

I stood.

"Now don't worry about this anymore. Go and enjoy the party."

I heard his boots on the stairs as I shuffled to the banister. Papa strode into the night, leaving the huge doors open behind him. I gazed down and saw the black dagger, sticking straight up out of the table. I shuddered. The front door swung in the breeze, creaking softly. I pulled the leather book out and stared at it.

But something had changed. Over the time code, an inky print smudged across the page—made by the finger of someone who had another copy of this exact same book. I ran to a writing hutch and spilled a bottle of quills. Dipping one in the ink, I began to write.

Is someone there?

Twenty Seven

Evan

Thursday
8:45 pm
26 hours, 4 minutes
until the falling

Blood covered me.

My fingers stuck together, tacky and wet. My cheek clung to the floor. Lifting my head, I rolled over. An unlit dome stretched above.

I looked closer at my hands. Not blood, just dirt and sweat. The burnt orange stool that Mazol made Henri stand on all night lay toppled on its side. I must have been out for hours, a restless sleep that took more than it gave. And of course, the dreams. I dreamed about falling, landing on the beach by my cottage. I dreamed about being someone great, like Cevo or Terillium. Of people bowing to me as I passed. Of being the hunter instead of the prey.

And then:

An old rickety cart drove through the castle gates into the jungles. In the cart's bed lay a splintered wooden crate with clumps of mud and dirt clinging to its side. A gravebox, freshly dug from the ground. It rattled. Someone was inside, someone who wasn't dead.

Who? Who was it inside the gravebox?
Pearl.
She's alive?
You tell me.

I gazed down the murky halls that lead away from the entrance hall. The Warts could come any moment, to give me another shot. I think they tried to kill me. I thought about what my father's letter said.

You will have to be much more aggressive now. The Spider alone may not be enough. If you have the ember, as I expect you do, that should save you.

They were following through with the plan, just like Terillium instructed. But I was getting stronger. They'd try to poison me again. They'd try harder next time, if the falling didn't happen first. I had a day to find Pearl, use the skull to find out who's causing the affliktion, lure the Warts into the jungle, leave Henri in charge, then, the falling.

My eyes fell on the lock on my wrist, and I found myself grinning. After what I did to Pearl, after I lifted a 500lb barrel of oil over my head, the Warts actually thought this little shackle could stop me?

Flexing my hand into a fist to break the shackle, I stopped. I might want them to think they can keep me locked up. I could let them keep me shackled if I need to get close to Mazol, breaking my chains when the time was right.

If you don't want to break the shackle, unlock it.

How?

Sapience.

I can't control it.

I've been practicing. Keeping busy while you sleep.

That's what worries me.

I stared at the lock, closed my eyes, and imagined its insides. The gears. The springs. The pins. The rivets. In my imagination, unlocking the shackle was easy. I flicked my finger. With a click, the cuff sprang free; metal slid across my skin.

I opened my eyes to find the shackle dangling free from the banister. Rubbing my wrist, I edged back, like it might reach out and bite me.

Am I still asleep, or is this real?

My mind turned to the last time those shackles were used. How many times had they held a Rosling captive under a lashing belt? As I watched, the shackles lifted into the air, pulling against the banister rail. Wood creaked, splintering as the handrail ripped apart. The shackles exploded into a thousand pieces. Metal shards fell all around the room, like rain on a tin roof.

So much for locking myself up later. And so much for not using sapience. I rose, tried to take a step, but my leg buckled. My brace was missing. Pain ripped through my bones. I needed Henri's help. But will she help me if I tell her where I think Mazol hid Pearl? What if I'm wrong and we find a corpse?

I ripped a spindle from the staircase to use as a cane. Limping through the castle's dingy passages, I found my way to the Caldroen's iron doors on the main level. I squinted through flooding firelight as my eyes adjusted to the glow. Moving from shadow to shadow, I edged closer to humming and whirring clankers.

"No breaks," Mazol said. "We're working through the night."

Several Roslings groaned.

"You don't need sleep," Mazol said.

Yesler flashed a toothy smile. "Yeah, it's all in your head."

Peeking around the door, I darted behind the Warts into a pipe-fitting room. I crawled through a duct that vented hot air away from the clankers into a room that I'd hidden in before. Peering through a rusted nickel grate, I spotted Henri.

Leaning close to Mazol, she spoke into his ear. A vision played through my mind:

Henri and Mazol and Little Saye laughed while I lay on the floor, a needle jabbed into my neck.

I squeezed the grate; the metal groaned. Henri turned away from Mazol and stared at the floor. He pulled her back to whisper in her ear. She tried to turn. He grabbed her face. Jerking away, she began lubing the aft-gears of a smoking and rattling clanker ten feet from where I hid.

"Pssst, Henri."

She jumped.

"Over here."

Squinting, she peered in my direction. I moved into the light.

"What are you doing here?" She glanced over her shoulder.

"Looking for you."

"You shouldn't have come."

"What were you talking to Mazol about?"

"Nothing," she said, her voice sharp enough to cut through iron. "What happened to you?"

"Yesler gave me something nasty."

"You should hide."

"Can you sneak away?"

She didn't respond.

"It's important." The nickel grate between us twisted, groaning. A bolt snapped with a ping of flying metal. I ducked as the bolt flew past my head, ricocheting down a vent pipe. Mazol's eyes darted in our direction. I ducked back into the shadows. Mazol stared right at me, but I was shrouded in darkness. After a moment, he turned away.

"I have to keep working," Henri said.

"Wait, please. I don't think Pearl's really dead."

"What are you talking about?"

"She's alive."

"You *know* she's alive? Or you *think* she's alive?"

"I can prove it; I just need to get to the Elusian."

Henri glanced at Mazol again. "Pearl got sick," she said. "That's all there is to it."

After you gave her the skull.

"So we should just give up on her?"

"It's called accepting reality."

"Is that what you and Mazol were talking about?"

She folded her arms.

"Mazol's a liar," I said. "He'll say anything to get us to do what he wants."

"You think I don't know that?"

"Just meet me in the hall in five minutes."

"But —"

I disappeared before she could argue anymore. As I made my way back to the hall, I wondered if Henri would help me if she knew we'd have to dig up Pearl's grave to find her. I pictured the faces of the erased Roslings. Little Saye. Anabelle. Lucy.

Ten minutes went by. I glanced at the clock in the hall again. Tick. Tock. Twelve minutes. Henri could have gone to Mazol about me. Maybe she put it all together then decided I was the killer. Maybe she was huddled with the Warts one room over, preparing another syringe.

Suddenly, out of the twilight, Henri appeared. I threw my arms around her, then stepped back, cheeks flushed.

"What's that for?" she said.

"I was starting to worry you wouldn't come."

"Thought about it." She laughed then stared at the floor. "Better get going."

She fell in beside me; lamp in hand, a stub-of-a-candle flickered inside like a clanker with a busted driveshaft. We headed toward the north wing of the castle, climbing stairs, rounding corners, passing rows and rows of veiled statues and stacks of furniture.

"So where did Mazol hide Pearl?" Henri said.

I didn't answer. We arrived at the base of the narrow stairs that lead to the Elusian. We stared up the cheerless stairwell. It seemed to grow longer and narrower.

I stepped to the first stair. "I... just need to get my little clanker. I'll be right back." I saw the Elusian, as if in a dream:

Flames and smoke swirled around me, shelves and chairs and broken beams lifted into the air, rock and iron shattered —

"Promise to wait outside when we get to the top?" I said.

"Why?"

"Don't ask that. Please."

She pursed her lips. Putting her arm around me, she took some weight off my bad leg. A minute later we stood on the landing. I opened the trap door inside the closet just large enough to slip through.

"What are you hiding from me?" she asked.

"Nothing." What *was* I hiding? The vision of the Elusian, it was just a dream. Those things I saw, they aren't possible, not even with sapience. I... I just... "I'm just tired of you snooping around all the time."

But I didn't mean that. I tried to smile. "I'll show you Saturday. I promise."

You're so cruel. You'll be gone by then.

I ducked through the closet and limped in the direction of the desk. My feet slipped along, like the floor was covered in a thick layer of dust. I could see no more than a few feet in any direction. Something sharp jabbed the bottom of my left foot. Wincing, I stepped sideways and stubbed my other toe.

I could feel eyes on me. The monster was waiting for me to fall asleep so he could take control of my body. Something shifted in the shadows.

The creak of wood on stone. I ignored it, bumped into something large in the middle of the room, then finally found the hutch with my knee. Cursing, I found the key and slid the drawer open.

This is where we met. Do you remember?

Feeling around inside, I searched for the leather bag. The drawer was empty. Panic rose in my chest. I searched again. Nothing. My hands moved to the desk. Ink bottle. A book. A stack of papers. I knocked a glass jar over; it cracked at my feet. Papers flew. I slammed the drawer shut, pinching my finger.

"What did you do with it!" I yelled into the darkness.

My hand found the edge of a leather cord under a few cuts of cloth. I traced the cord to a small leather sack. The rubrics. I exhaled.

I started to shut the drawer, but my hand found the old book. I held it close and found the time code. Twenty-six hours. I shoved my finger in the bottle of ink and wiped over the time. Now it was just a sooty splotch. Turning to leave, I saw a flash of light at the door. Henri stood inside the room, staring at the floor, the little candle lamp shaking in her hand. My eyes darted around the Elusian, stopping on the spot where Henri stared. Something on the floor; I couldn't quite make it out.

I squinted.

A list of names.

Twenty Eight

Cevo

Tearing a mammal into four pieces is
like disarticulating a wishbone.

Or like an angry crowd on the edge of losing control. You never know which way it is going to go. The people simmered, but perhaps they had more sense than I gave them credit for. Perhaps they did remember me after all.

Mahalelel kept his distance. It had been 29 years, 324 days since I lost my temper with him. Since I last broke my vow. Not once had I lost my temper since then. Not once. This is the new Cevo, Mahalelel. What do you think of me? This is Cevo in control. Cevo with vision. I have seen the world and have seen the future. One where I am the only sapient left alive. Father really did love the others best. But I will be the one alive in the end. Then I will carry this limitless power to my grave, this secret that the world should never have uncovered. Because only I have the self control. Only I can handle the power without pain and destruction raining down on all around me.

So maybe I had given myself a few breaks from the vow in the last thirty years. They were short, inconsequential. And only once or twice. What did it matter? The witnesses have been recalled to their maker. Mahalelel knew nothing of those breaks. He only knew he did not want to stand witness to another.

Greenskins surrounded the crowd and edged forward, spears lowered. Eagles large enough to carry away a child circled overhead, sensing the pending meal. The execution proconsul stared at me.

"What are you waiting for?" I shouted.

Shuffling, he glanced at the crowd, their gritted teeth, their smoldering murmur. Worthless porcus; this proconsul will be chiseling rock with the rest of the slaves by the time the sun sets tonight.

"Lynch the man first if it soothes your conscience." I checked my pocket watch. The proconsul gave a command. Men secured ropes to horses and cinched knots. The proconsul cracked his whip. Horses whinnied, lurching forward. I heard the springy sound of a plucked cithara. The man screamed, then, with a gushing pop, fell silent. I cleaned under my fingernails, peering through the balusters to see which appendage hung from the man's torso. The right leg this time. That makes it 233 for the right leg to 205 for the left. The arms are far less likely. I surmise this has something to do with the tendons and joints in the shoulder being smaller and weaker than the hip.

Eagles swooped down, pecking the man's entrails like men husked piscatus on fishing schooners. Guards batted them away, but the birds were too many. Most of the jura's remains were soon gone.

I moved to the edge of my seat. "Now the girl."

The proconsul squirmed like he had nepa crawling in his pants. He glanced sideways at the crowd as his men tied Hagnus's ropes to the horses.

"It ain't right!" someone from the crowd yelled.

"You gotta let her go!"

I jumped to my feet. "Ignore them."

The proconsul finally cracked his whip. The ropes went tight, the same plucked-string-note as with the man, but no pop.

Hagnus vibrated, limbs stretched, eyes closed. Lines of concentration formed on her forehead. The proconsul cracked his whip again. Four Clydesdales heaved. The greenskins slapped the horses. One reared up, straining against the rope. It snapped. The horse galloped into the screaming crowd.

Using her now free hand, Hagnus ripped the gag from her mouth, eyes locked on me. "Do you wish you'd taken the time to see me now?" she whispered. I heard her as clearly as if she stood next to me. I felt the warmth of Hagnus's skin with my outstretched fingers, turned her head a little left, a little right, so she knew I could snap her in two. How I wanted to twist that little neck, but I had to circumscribe. I must keep the crowd ignorant.

It is time for you to commit suicide, little Hagnus. Too bad you do not have time to write a note. I made her free hand rise, grabbing the length of dangling rope. She fought me. Stronger than I guessed she was capable of. But not strong enough.

Hagnus wrapped the rope around her neck again and again.

"Help—"

Forcing her mouth shut, I felt her voice reverberate into my skin. I tried to make her hand release, to let her body fall. She resisted. I leaned over the handrail, concentrated on her fingers, focused on bending her muscles to my will. Two words escaped from her lips.

"Evan Burl!"

My equilibrium tipped. "Quid dicis—" I steadied myself on the handrail. "What did you say?"

She gasped. "I know you're looking for him."

"So what if I am?"

"If you let me live, I'll take you to Evan Burl."

Twenty Nine

Evan

Thursday
9:30 pm
25 hours, 19 minutes
until the falling

Henri stared at the floor.

Her lamp speckled the room with faded orange glow. Burnt furniture, destroyed collections, ashes and soot blanketed the room. She didn't seem to notice the pictures carved on walls and furniture—like ancient cave drawings—the same images, repeated over and over, of how three Roslings met their grizzly ends. A girl hung by her neck out the window. A body in the furnace. A lump of legs and arms curled on the floor.

I limped to her side, tucking the book in my belt behind me. I thought about my bloody fingers, the sand and grime I found under my nails this morning, after a six hour blackout. I knew who wrote this list of names, this list of twelve. This list with the first three names crossed out.

— ~~Little Saye~~ —
— ~~Anabelle~~ —
— ~~Lucy~~ —
Pearl
Henrietta
Gertrude
Parkrose
Haller
Roxhill
Othella
Vashion
Ravenna

Three dead. Nine to go.

And Henri's name was next after Pearl.

A voice in my ear.

This looks like the list of a murderer.

I tried to lift her chin. "Hey."

"Where did this come from?"

I caught a glimpse of an engraving behind her, Lucy staring up at the ceiling, her arms spread open as flames consumed her.

You're quite the artist.

A migraine burrowed into the bones above my eyes. "I don't know..." I watched her. "Henri, we don't have time to sort this out now."

"What's there to sort? My name's right there." She pointed. "I'm next."

If you fall asleep.

"Not now—" I started to say to the monster. Henri glared at me. "I mean... the list could be anything."

Why don't you give her a rubric to keep her safe? That helped so well with the Lucy and Anabelle and Pearl...

Soft laughter echoed from the stairwell as I pulled the clanker rubric from my pocket. "I want to show you something." I held the rubric out to her. "Pearl needs us."

Shoulders hanging, she looked. Above the word *rubric* it read:

The Blood Pumpery

She held the flicking candle closer as I turned the rubric over. Her back straightened. "What is it?"

"Give me your hand."

She jumped at my touch. I placed the rubric in her palm.

"What?"

"Do you feel it?"

She shook her head.

"It's supposed to beat. Like a heart." I squeezed the rubric, rubbing it harder and harder. She put her hand on my arm.

I pulled away. "It just needs to warm up." I breathed on it, rubbing more.

"Maybe Mazol wasn't lying about Pearl."

I rubbed until my hands were raw. Spiders crawled inside me—I didn't want the clanker to beat. The nightmare had worked me over good, convinced me Pearl was alive; so if he was right about her, he was right about me being the murderer too.

"Did you hear that?" Henri pressed the clanker to her ear.

I grabbed at it. She twisted away.

"Give it back—"

"Shhhh." Thump, thump. The spiders inside me turned into hornets.

I told you.

My migraine spread.

When are you going to start believing me?

A tiny light grew inside the rubric until it saturated Henri's fingers. The beams burst through her skin, revealing the life that pumped through her veins. Sparks escaped from the rubric; burning sawdust floating around us.

"What is that sound?" Henri said.

"Pearl." My voice was as weak as Pearl's heart.

"How did you know it would beat?"

"I was worried she's be next—"

"Because she's next on the list," Henri said, her voice quiet.

The list you wrote.

I nodded. "I gave her a rubric that's connected to the clanker."

Tell her about me.

"Because of a dream. I just had a feeling—"

Coward.

"Everyone dies," Henri said. "Maybe it's just my time."

She's right.

I took her shaking hand in mine. "Don't say that."

You can't save her.

"Does it matter?" Henri said.

But you can save yourself.

"No—" I said to the monster.

Henri's eyes went wet.

"Of course it matters." I wiped clammy fingers on my pants then pulled her closer. "Do you remember the closet? You said you believe."

She gazed up.

"You were right."

"Of course I was right." She stared at me a long moment. "Let's run away. We'll get the Roslings, leave tonight—"

Put her out of her misery.

I rubbed my forehead, trying to stem the pain in my skull. "It's not safe."

If you can't do it, I will.

"It's not safe here either," she said.

"We need to find Pearl. The rubric I gave her will tell us what's causing the affliktion. After tomorrow, you'll all be safe here."

"What happens tomorrow?"

"I just have a feeling it will all be over soon."

"But this room. This list..." Henri's eyes fixed on my hands, the crusted blood and the ground fingernails. She covered her mouth and whispered, "It's you. You did this."

"I don't know. I don't remember—"

Henri edged away. "But how could you know who will die next? How could you make this list unless—"

"I'm the murderer? Yeah, thanks, I thought of that."

"But—"

"You're right. I've been blacking out, waking up places I don't remember going. So it could be me..."

"I don't understand."

"I'm not safe—that's why we can't run away. Not until I prove it's Mazol."

We fell silent. My head throbbed. A vision of Henri's face struck me, right after Yesler jabbed me with the needle. 'You're not who you think you are,' Henri said. Or was it, 'you're not as awake as you think you are'? The memory was so faded; I couldn't even be sure it happened.

I clutched her hand. "I'm scared Henri."

"I am too." She paused. "What do we do now?"

"We use this clanker to find Pearl. It'll grow stronger the closer we get."

"What about Mazol? I've been gone too long. They'll know we're up to something."

I thought again of her quiet conversation with Mazol in the Caldroen.

She'll sell your life for a loaf of bread.

"This is our only chance," I said. "We have to go now."

She nodded. We padded noiselessly down long hallways and stairs. Henri limped through a beam of moonlight. She massaged her back, rubbed her eyes. Some intuition deep inside me screamed, telling me what was wrong, but I was too deaf to hear. I found myself fumbling through the bag of rubrics in my pocket. A fragment of the nightmare with Pearl's gravebox came back to me.

Dravus drove his old rickety cart through the castle gates into the jungles. In the cart's bed lay a splintered wooden crate with clumps of mud and dirt clinging to its side.

I stopped. "Did anyone come to the castle today?"

Henri turned away from me. "I don't know..."

"What about Dravus?"

She didn't answer. She wouldn't look me in the eyes.

"Henri?"

"I said no one came."

She walked on. I hurried to catch up. In the flickering candlelight, I kept an eye on Henri, her sunken face, her pale skin crossed with veins. I stumbled on a stair. The book fell out of my belt. Henri swooped it up.

"Give that here, Henri."

"Is this really it? The letter?"

"It belongs to me." I tried to grab it.

She held it out slowly; its pages flapping open. "Why don't you trust me?"

I snapped it from her. As I moved to shove it back in my belt, I caught a glimpse of large letters scrawled across a blank page as it flipped by.

Is someone there?

I found the page, read the words again. "Where's the nearest writing cabinet?"

"I think there's one in that big, blue room." She pointed down the hall.

I limped to it, threw open the door, and tore through the hutch until I found a quill and ink.

Henri appeared at the door. "What's going on?"

"Someone is sending a message."

Thirty

Claire

I stared at the book, willing words to appear.

As I waited, I took the quill and ink bottle outside to the balcony that surveyed the courtyard. Music and laughter and the clanking of dishes rang in my ears. I sat on the edge of a wicker chair and read the letters again. Minutes went by and nothing. I'd almost given up, was about to shut the book when it happened. Lit by moonlight, letters formed on the page.

Who are you?

Someone was writing to me—someone with horrible penmanship—but someone was writing to me! I grabbed the quill and spilled the ink. Dipping the pen in the puddle on the floor, I wrote back.

My name is Claire Amadeus. This book belongs to my father. What's your name?

I waited. A moment later:

Evan Burl.

I slammed the book shut. This can't really be happening. Can it? I opened it, slowly, squinting, afraid I might scare the letters away. New words were waiting.

Terillium is my father too. Is it possible, I mean, do you think you're my sister?

My chest thumped as I replied.

I want to help you. I'm trying to stop Papa from hurting you.

Feeling eyes watching, I looked up. All I could see from my chair was the wall Papa built to protect us from the jungle. Invisible ants crawled up my leg. The jungles were growing more dangerous every year, especially at night. I wondered what prowled out there at this very moment. I wondered what was watching me.

Something grim moved across the courtyard toward me. I leaned forward. Orbs appeared, two of them. A pair of eyes. They saw me too; I swear they measured me, then blinked and were gone. The shadow faded through a door into our house.

Thirty One

Evan

Thursday
9:42 pm
25 hours, 7 minutes
until the falling

We stared at the book.

My words hung like an unwanted confession of love.

What is the falling?

The wall clock ticked off a full minute—never had sixty ticks taken so long. The sound was soon replaced in my mind with Pearl's heartbeat, growing fainter with each passing second. I stood. "We better keep moving."

Henri nodded.

We left the blue room.

"You have a sister," Henri said.

I smiled, but only because it seemed like the right thing to do. We arrived at a narrow door. Henri rattled the handle. Locked. Her eyes lit. "Can you break it down?"

I wrapped my fingers around the knob.

"I already tried," she said.

I peered inside the lock with my mind, trying to remember the sensation of the unlocked shackles. I heard a tiny click. Pressure from the stored up sapience in my veins released. My migraine all but evaporated. Turning the handle, I pushed the door open. It creaked long.

I thought you weren't using sapience?

I forgot—my instincts had taken over.

Keep it up. I'll be running that body of yours by the end of the night.

"But I just..." Henri said.

I coughed. "Must've been stuck."

She stepped through the doorway, glanced over her shoulder. "Are you coming?"

I stared at Henri, trying not to imagine Mazol whispering in her ear.

Use pain. Make her tell you what she's up to with Mazol.

But I want to hold her, to feel her lips on mine.

You can't stay.

I have to get used to the idea of being alone. Of never seeing Henri again. I moved to pass her, but she stopped me, her hand on my chest. Could she feel the pounding? I tried to push past. She moved her hand to my face, forcing me to look in her eyes, so close I could feel her breath.

154

"We" — I swallowed — "have to go."

She leaned up, so our lips almost touched. "I'm sorry Evan."

I didn't breath. She kissed me on the cheek then took my hand. A moment later, I think my legs began to move, one in front of the other. Walking.

We passed through the next room and the one after that. Henri's hand so small, calloused, soft. Trembling. I wanted to live in that moment forever. But something began to twist inside me. Her hand hardened. Her skin chilled.

What's Henri sorry about?

Don't ruin my last few hours with Henri. Please.

What's she doing behind your back?

I searched her face for a clue. She stared straight ahead, her eyes wet at the corners. I tried to remember the kiss, to concentrate on how her skin felt so soft against mine, but I couldn't stop the images of her and Mazol from flooding my mind. Her skin felt rough now. I scanned her again. Her face, frozen; and her tears turned to flaking chrome.

Thirty Two

Claire

I burst into my sister's room.

Anastasia stood in front of a three-sided mirror, holding up a dress. She glared at me.

"I need to tell you something."

She shoved past me and fell onto a velvet sofa. "Look at me, I'm so fat."

"Ani—"

She yawned. "I think I ate too much."

I twisted the skin under her arm.

"Owww!" Anastasia clutched my hair, forcing me to lean over her.

"I only wanted you to listen."

Anastasia shoved me away. "You're a freak."

A thud came from the hallway.

"Did you hear that?" I imagined the shadow gliding down the passage, searching for me. Anastasia returned to the mirror, staring at herself this way and that. I joined her, the small book in my hand. "There's something I have to tell you about Papa."

Anastasia slipped an orange dress over her head. "Ouuu, it's pretty." She turned to admire the view of her back. The dress shimmered bright orange and red. She took the second dress off the hanger, shoving it at me. "Don't be an ungrateful pig."

"I don't want to wear that stupid thing."

"Put it on now!" Terisma had found her way into the room with us, I could feel her cold breath.

"Fine," I said. "Just listen to me."

Anastasia took a brush to her hair.

I wriggled out of my clothes. "I overheard Mother and Papa arguing."

"Your dress is brighter than mine, isn't it?"

"I found this book, and I've been writing to this boy named—"

"It's not fair; you always get the better gifts."

I whacked her with the book. "Would you shut it!"

Anastasia spun around and sank her nails into my arm.

"Stop, please, it's important."

She squeezed harder. I felt a trickle of blood on my arm. Grabbing a wooden hanger from the rack, I raised it above my head.

Anastasia's face turned to ice. "You wouldn't dare." Memories of tortured and twisted animal bodies flashed through my mind. But I didn't lower the hanger. Ani's eyes narrowed. "You think you're not afraid, don't you?"

"I'm not."

Anastasia shoved me into the mirror. I toppled over it with a crash, cutting my hands on broken glass.

She whispered in my ear. "Let's see if Terisma wants to play." The raven circle of her eyes doubled in size, nearly swallowing the white. Muffled sounds from the party outside seemed to grow in my ears, though the windows were shut tight.

"I'm not afraid."

"Liar."

"It's you who's frightened."

"Of a tatter like you?"

"Afraid of what I can do."

"Are you gonna wipe boogers on me?"

I shoved past her and pulled a piece of glass from my skin. "I can make you hurt. Burn you with fire. If I wanted."

Anastasia rolled her eyes.

The door creaked. My eyes snapped to the sound. It swung slowly open. A figure flashed past in the dark hall. I thought I heard beating wings. I pulled a lamp off the wall and crept closer. Lifting the lantern high, I peered into the passage. The shadow was gone.

Pushing the door shut, I checked that the handle clicked into place, then reached up and locked the bolt just in case. I found the book lying open on the floor and slipped it in the belt of my dress, then turned to Anastasia. "Papa isn't who we think he is—"

"No. I want to see your magic first."

I hesitated. "I can't do it right now. It only works when I really need it."

"Stultus."

"Fine. Stand back." I focused on Anastasia's bed.

"You're not going to burn *me*?"

"Don't want to hear you whine about how Fredrick doesn't want to kiss you anymore."

Anastasia held her nose. "Your breath reeks. Brush your teeth."

"Stand over there." I waved her back. "No. Further." I narrowed my focus so everything beyond the bed's white wooden frame went blurry.

Anastasia laughed. "You look stupid."

"Shhh."

"We could be eating candy and pie right now." Anastasia sighed. "Hey, they have the cake out there."

I spread my arms full, paused, then clapped my hands hard. Two tea cups rattled on a shelf beside me and something went bump, like a chest slamming shut. Did my magic make those sounds? Or the shadow?

Hair stood up on my skin as I felt someone's touch, a hand moving slowly up my arm, or a soft breeze. I backed against the window, folded my arms tight, checked the door. Shut. Locked. No... The lock was open. I couldn't think, did I remember to bolt it? Did Ani unlock the door when I wasn't looking?

"Can we go now?" Anastasia said.

I searched the room. "Is someone there?"

"Who are you talking to?"

I shook my head.

Anastasia pointed out the open window. "They're cutting the cake without us."

"Did you open this?"

"You did."

"The window was shut when I came in."

"What does it matter?"

I looked out, searching for the shadow. Papa noticed us. He waved. Then I saw it. Above the stairs, the shadow crept across the balcony. Or did it fly? It seemed to take the shape of wings. A huge crow. It could have passed through Ani's room and crawled out to the ledge through the window. Watching it enter the house again, I grabbed Ani. "Look!"

"What?"

"Something dark, like someone wearing a midnight cloak." I pointed. "Right there."

"Do you ever get tired of making stuff up?"

"I'm not. I swear."

"It was just a servant."

I sniffed. "Do you smell that?"

Ani sucked air through her nose.

"I think something is burning," I said.

"You mean those?" Anastasia pointed at a cluster of candles hanging from the wall below us.

I pushed the window open further, wincing from the cut on my hand. Staring out, I remembered the knife on the desk at the bottom of the stairs, right below where the shadowed had just reentered the house. I didn't touch it. Papa wanted me to take it, to finish off Evan Burl. But I didn't take it. I will never touch that blade, not if it means saving my own life. But the shadow might have found it. And if he used it, if he used it to hurt my Papa, it would be my fault.

My back felt suddenly warm. Crackling and popping behind me. Chest pounding, I turned. My face blistered hot. I tugged at my sister's dress. "Ani."

"Cut it out."

"The bed is on fire!"

Thirty Three

Evan

Thursday
9:55 pm
24 hours, 54 minutes
until the falling

Forty foot walls of rusted bronze and
glass rose around us.

The greenhouses. They were beautiful when I was a child, five buildings in a row like crystal soldiers defending the castle against a bloodless city rising up beyond the panes of beaten glass. And inside, all the food I could eat: bananas and açaí berries and avocados and coconuts. But the fruit withered long ago. Nothing edible had grown in years. Then, typhoons struck Daemanhur three seasons ago, thirty-eight days of ceaseless torrents. The castle's thick windows survived; the greenhouse didn't stand a chance.

Henri and I stepped into a downpour. Rivers of rain dumped down in pillars where the roof was no more. She shielded her candle lamp—a tiny stub of wax that looked near to giving up the ghost—as we splashed through the undergrowth.

"What do you think you'd be doing right now," I said, "if you never fell to Daemanhur?"

"Not this."

"Do you have the dreams anymore? Of your life before falling?"

She shook her head, a little too fast.

"But your mother, you said you see her sometimes, like you're hiding under a deck and she's running over the top of you. Like she was scared of something."

"I have no memories of my mother."

"You told me just last month—" I cut short, deciding to let it go. We moved slowly, walking the long way around cobwebs and broken shelves and clay pots and root balls that seemed to move like snakes, slithering against our bodies as we passed. Eyes blinked at us from the mist. I watched carefully where I placed my feet, stepping over splinters or thorns or broken glass. A tarantula the size of a rat swung in front of my face. Henri bumped into me, saw the spider, then shrieked. It crawled to a branch and joined several others feeding on what looked like a raccoon. Dozens of tarantulas encircled us as we ducked under their webs and made our way to a narrow garden shed built against the outside wall.

The door kiltered, half fallen off, clinging to the broken brick wall only by its bottom hinge. If I remembered right, there was a rack of tools in the back of the shed. Shovels. Taking the candle from Henri, I held it to the darkness inside. The light flickered, then extinguished into a lonely stream of smoke. I stepped to the threshold and reached into the cavity.

Henri pulled me back. "Evan, don't!"

"I have to go in."

"What if something's in there?"

I felt nothing but air. Twilight enveloped me, the kind of pitch that made seconds feel like death. The back wall was too far to reach. I stepped in, guiding myself with my hands. Rain pounded against the tin roof. Something clunked behind me. I froze. "That you Henri?"

Her voice was muffled. "Was what me?"

"Never mind," I said to myself.

I found the back wall and the rack of tools then felt the shape of tool heads and the shovel I'd come for. Returning to Henri, I saw the lines of fear written on her face.

"What's that got to do with Pearl?"

I pushed it into the ground and pulled out a scoop of mud. The bite wound on my arm seared with pain.

"Yeah, I know it's for digging," she said.

"Where exactly did you think we would find Pearl?"

"I don't know. Not buried. What if she's—"

"Dead? You heard the heart beat."

"That could have been someone else. How do you know it was Pearl?"

"I'll just do it myself."

"Mazol wouldn't kill the Roslings. It doesn't make sense."

"You and him are getting pretty close, aren't you?"

"What? Of course not." She turned away from me.

"What were you two talking about then?"

"Nothing. When?"

"You know when."

"In the Caldroen? That was nothing. He was just... telling me to..."

"To what?" I moved into her gaze, but she turned away.

"To finish sweeping up before I left for the night."

"You do that every night."

Henri scratched her neck. "He was reminding me."

"You expect me to believe that?"

"That's not the point. I mean, even if Mazol wanted to kill us, how does he do it? We're Roslings. We're supposed to be immortal, remember?"

"Obviously you're not."

"You think he hung Little Saye up in the rafters? You think he threw Anabelle in the Caldroen? You think he—"

"It's either him or me..." Or Dravus. Henri turned into a wall whenever I tried to talk to her about the things I did with Dravus. I think she's jealous of our relationship. So I don't mention him when I can help it.

"What if the affliktion is just a sickness?" she said. "Remember when the fruit trees all died. Do you think Mazol did that too?"

"It's possible."

"You always do this. You let your imagination get the best of you. You dream up things that aren't there."

I wished I could say she was wrong, but my imagination had gotten me in a lot of trouble over the years. Once, when food was missing from the pantries, I was convinced Yesler was stealing it. Henri and I snuck into his room to find evidence, got caught, and earned two lashes each from my uncle. Another time, I thought there was a savage loose in the castle. We set traps each night for a week, but in the end, all we caught was Ballard. Mazol made us both sit in one of the traps for three whole days. Then I discovered the savage was a scrawny ebony cat.

"I didn't realize you've been keeping score." Stiffening my neck, I tried to step pass Henri, but she moved in front of me.

"I'm not letting you go out there alone," she said.

"You heard Pearl's heartbeat."

"That could be anything."

I imagined prying open the gravebox, finding Pearl's stiff, rotting corpse staring up at us. Would I be happy to find her stiff? Relieved that the monster was wrong? The thought made my stomach ache. My head began to throb. I sat down on a pile of clay pots to rub my temples.

Henri sat beside me. After a moment, she took the shovel from me. "We'll try to find her. I mean, if you really think she's alive, we can't just leave her out there."

I attempted a smile, but couldn't find the strength. "Thanks."

"We're gonna need another shovel."

"Right." I limped to the shed, hesitated in the threshold, standing on the edge of its darkness.

Henri scratched her neck. "Be careful."

A crash. Something inside the shed clanked against the wall, then fell toward me. A rake handle splashed into the mud at my feet. I braced my hands on either side of the door, leaned into the unlit shed.

"Hello?"

No answer. I lifted my foot to step inside.

"Evan, no—"

Something dashed out of the dark between my legs. Henri screamed. I scrambled backward, toppling into a mud puddle. I wiped mud from my face. Slowly, a jackblue came into focus. He perched on a stump, twitching his little rabbit whiskers, staring at me, then dove into the undergrowth.

Henri helped me from the puddle. I managed to find a second shovel without any more harmless animals attacking me. Outside the greenhouses, the rain poured down. I wondered if Mazol could see us from the castle as we sloshed through the courtyard in the muggy fog. Or maybe he was hiding out there somewhere in the night, another syringe in hand.

We traced along the edge of the longgrass, toward the mournful outline of the great balizia tree against the storming sky. Pike used to love climbing that tree; that's why Mazol buried him there. The Roslings are buried there now—on the shore of the lake between the courtyard and the perished city.

Screams echoed from the gates. Shades must have heard us coming—shadows of humans, teeth chattering, torn skin, brown and lurid from mud and bruises and dried blood. Mazol said Shades were people who had become addicted to mums, hallucinogens that combined every possible joy into a single moment, but crushed you under an avalanche of anguish when the effects wore off.

Shades moved through the jungle in packs, scraping the final months of their existence from the muck. When their tongues got so swollen they could no longer scream, their faces turned white and sweaty. Then the retching began—that meant they only had a few hours to live. Sometimes they died intertwined in the portcullis like brambles, holding out hope until the last that one of us might offer one last shot of mums. Or that we might end their misery with the edge of a sickle. They never lasted more than two weeks. Sometimes we called dead things—or things that were about to die—two week Shades.

I tried to ignore the howling cries as we plodded through the mud, thinking instead of Claire. My sister. I wondered if she'd written anything new in the book, if she could give me a clue about what waited for me in the falling.

Henri lagged further behind, grimacing when she put weight on her right leg. I tried to help her along, but I could barely walk myself, even with the shovel to lean on. It seemed to take an hour to arrive at the edge of the lake. Five graves lay in a row under the great balizia tree: one named for Pike, three with bundles of fresh tulips and the last, a fresh, unmarked mound of mud.

"You think she's really down there," Henri said.

I pulled out the clanker rubric. It beat loudly.

"One way to find out." I pulled up a clump of mud. My arm screamed in pain. Henri glanced back at the castle, silhouetted against angry clouds, all windows clouded but two. Yellow eyes, flickering. Daemanhur was always watching.

We worked in silence for a while—only the screams of Shades and drenching rain to keep us company. But soon, others joined us. Creatures watched from the tree canopy above, leaping from branch to branch to get a closer look, screeching.

The pain I felt throughout my body was unbearable. I dreamed of using sapience to finish the digging. But I forced myself on, gritting my teeth as I pulled another scoop of mud from the hole.

I glanced up and noticed a long, thin leather bag hanging from Henri's belt. "What's that?"

Henri turned sideways, hiding the bag from my view. "Nothing. Just a..."

"Bag?"

"Yeah. Just a bag."

"Right," I said. "Is there anything in it?"

She pushed her shovel deep in the mud and flung the scoop out. "Can we just get this over with?"

"Fine. Forget about it."

She reached up to push a wet strand of hair from her eyes. Pulling the collar of her shirt down, she scratched her neck for what must have been the hundredth time. I wiped rain from my eyes and squinted to see what looked like a mark on her skin.

Not a mark—a rash. How could I have been so blind? The list was right. Henri was next.

Henri had the affliktion.

Henri would be a two week Shade by morning.

Thirty Four

Cevo

Animal heads covered the walls.

Elk. Polar bears. Leopards. Elephants. I did not slaughter the animals myself, of course. Hunting is positively boorish. I order them in from a wonderful taxidermist overseas. The first time I saw a whole row of large, stuffed animal heads hanging in my den I felt so... exhilaratus.

Taxidermy is so virile.

And now, seeing my old friends again after thirty years was like a family reunion. And back in my own home again. Terillium bequeathed the mansion to me, but the city had claimed this place as their ruling chambers after I left. Mahalelel would live here from now on; he was going to have to get used to living alone.

I noticed one of the mounts was missing. Second from the left, above the door that led to the ruling chamber. Mahalelel always hated that alligator; I bet he sold it the day I left town. I stared at the empty space. "That is where I will put Evan's head. What do you think about that?"

Hagnus did not respond. We faced each other, sitting in two large leather chairs—she was bound at her wrists and ankles.

Tapping my fingers, I sighed. "The problem I have, Hagnus, is that I cannot trust your information. The only option I have is to suffocate you. It is not personal, I hope you understand."

"That's a comfort."

They key to negotiating is striking the right balance between fear and hope. First, you make your adversary believe her worst fears are about to become a reality. For example, a slow, painful death. Or, even more effective, the slow, painful death of a loved-one. Then you allow a seed of hope to foster—that she possesses the opportunity to avoid this imminent reality. People will do almost anything to maintain that shred of hope.

"If I had some way to verify the truth of your claims," I said, "that would be quite another matter. But my usual methods of getting what I want—variations on the motivational tool known as pain—do not work when I want to know what is inside a human head. People will say anything when their fingers are being smashed with a hammer..." My voice trailed off as I became caught up with the thought of what came next: my hands wrapped around her throat, watching life flicker from her eyes—

"What are you doing to the people?" she said. "I heard servants in the hall; they said you're executing children."

"After you were cut from the scaffolding this morning, I gave the people of El Qir the opportunity of a lifetime. Volunteer to work in my mines or be skinned alive. Four people chose to be skinned. After that, the rest followed my guards obediently below ground. So, I do not understand why you would ask if I am executing children. That would be counterproductive, would it not? Why would I harm my own employees?"

"Slaves?"

I frowned. "Is there a difference?"

"Employees don't get slaughtered if they take a personal day."

"Sounds like a wretched concept."

"Only for you."

"Oh, an idealist? You are beginning to remind me of my late wife."

"She was that smart?"

"I must retain the right to terminate the bad stock. How else could I get anything done?"

"They're not animals."

I found my pulse quickening. Hagnus seemed so familiar... But I had made a vow. I could not let this woman, this very young women, get her hooks into me. "Do not romanticize them."

"They have families."

My smile grew. "Even the little ones can dig."

"What are they doing—"

"Too many questions. I will not be interrogated." I clamped her mouth shut with sapience and smiled. "Let us enjoy each other's silence for a while, shall we?"

She glared at me, large round eyes boiling over. Fear, yes, but she was also excited. I was not surprised. This is a common occurrence with women, young and old. The way she breathed, how her lips parted when I spoke. I slid into the chair next to her. She seemed even younger. Yet children cannot master sapience like Hagnus could. I gestured to her wrists. "Why are you still bound?" I released my hold on her voice.

She gasped, sucked in air. "I thought you weren't using sapience."

I eyed her suspiciously. "What would you know about that?" It was just Hagnus and I. No one had to know, certainly not Mahalelel. And it was just a little bit, nothing like splashing her guts all over the wall.

Mahalelel burst through the door. "This can't go on."

"Do not be rude. Hagnus and I were in the middle of a conversation."

The snake-like straps uncoiled from her wrists and ankles and slithered to the ground.

To Hagnus I mouthed the word: "Impressive."

She rolled her eyes.

"Release the people," Mahalelel said. "Or I'll —"

"Be thankful brother, because I am going to give you everything you desire. I know you lust for ruling this cesspool of a city."

He leaned forward. "You'd make me Chancellor?"

"As soon as the mines are in order. You honestly believed I wanted to rule this city?"

Mahalelel nodded at Hagnus. "She's of your kind, isn't she?" Mahalelel scooted his chair, increasing the distance between them. She kissed at him.

Mahalelel curled up his nose. "Send her away. We have business."

"Hagnus is not long for this world. She is no threat to us."

"Why are you letting her live?" Mahalalel said.

"Funny, I was just wondering the same thing about you," Hagnus said.

"Our brother Terillium did something foolish. He bequeathed his first and most precious Sacrist, the Spider, to Evan Burl. Hagnus claims to have information on where I can find it."

"When will it be enough for you? How much power does one person need?"

"Evan Burl received the Spider in hopes that the boy would grow up to rule over the Cultures once Terillium was dead. Our brother believed sapience could be used for good, if it was kept in check by someone powerful enough to quench those who got out of hand. But Terillium was wrong. Sapience must be blotted out of history. Not even the Three Families can be allowed to live."

Hagnus edged closer, her hands hidden under the table. "What about you?"

I imagined her slipping a skewer from within her dress, a blade she'd managed to hide in the scraps of cloth that had hung from her body during the execution. I imagined her sliding the razor edge across my throat.

"After removing all remnants of the atrocity my father discovered, I will take sapience with me to the grave."

"So where is he?" Mahalelel said. "Where is Evan Burl?"

"He could be anywhere. I do not know how old he is, or if he knows the power of the Spider."

"I can tell you," Hagnus said.

I ignored her. "Mahalelel, you will rule over the people of El Qir. Give them mums to keep them docile. You will not need guards once they are hooked; they will do whatever you command to keep their addiction fed. We will use Terillium's clankers to create a third Sacrist, in case I am unable to find the Spider."

"What of the Crow?"

"Missing for hundreds of years. It may not even exist."

Hearing the slide of metal on skin, I glanced at Hagnus. Her hand moved under the table. She froze. I swung my hand. The table flew sideways. In Hagnus's hand was a black shiv.

"You came here to assassinate me?"

"I have my own vision for a better world. It doesn't include you."

"You have nothing on Evan Burl?"

"He—"

"You have been wasting my time?" I watched her grasp at the invisible fingers contracting around her neck. She gasped. The coal blade fell to the groundwork.

"Did you actually think..." I stepped toward her. "You did; I can see it. You actually believed you could come into my own house and kill *me*."

Mahalelel moved to the door.

"Stay." I slammed the door shut. "I must remove every last remnant of Hagnus's kind, and you are going to help me little brother."

She searched for the clenching fingers, but there was nothing to find. She gasped. "You let the others live—"

"Who?"

"The children."

"What are you talking about?"

"You sent them to Daemanhur. The babies."

"Tell me what you know!" I squeezed harder.

"That's where you'll find Evan Burl. That's where Terillium sent him."

"Impossible."

She flicked her fingers. A scrap of parchment appeared between them. I summoned it.

Evan Burl's falling
Daemanhur Castle
10:49 in the evening on March 27 1522

I shook the note at her. "Where did you get this?"

Hagnus's face went purple. I loosened my grip.

"Terillium put you up to this, didn't he?"

She gurgled. I released her. She collapsed.

"I..." She sucked in air. "I stole it from him."

"Why did you wait to show me?"

"I wanted to see what you knew."

"You were going to kill me," I said.

"I wasn't, I swear."

"I saw the blade. Did Terillium make that too? He said he was crafting one. A knife that could eradicate even the most powerful sapient. And now it is mine."

"No, I-I wanted to make a deal with you."

I slapped her. "This note does nothing for me without a rubric."

"That's where you sent the children?" Mahalelel said. "To Daemanhur?"

"Terillium set me up. It was his idea." Daemanhur castrum is the place I most want to forget, and now, the place I most desperately need to get to.

A trickle of blood ran from Hagnus's nose. "I can help you get there."

"There's nothing you can do for me."

Hagnus snapped her fingers. A vialus rubric appeared, floating above her palm.

I pulled at it. She closed her fingers.

"Where did you get that?"

"I have a deal for you," she said.

"That rubric is inanimate. It is no good to me."

"We both know you can activate it."

"So, is that your deal? The rubric for your life?"

"I want to be your partner."

I laughed. "I do not have partners."

"You do now."

"I can just annihilate you and take the vialus."

"If you kill me, you never find out what I know about Evan Burl."

"I know everything."

"Terillium hid this from you. It's your brother's darkest secret."

"How can you possibly know what I know and do not know?"

She smiled. "It's obvious."

"Enlighten me."

"If you knew what I know about Evan Burl, you'd be far more afraid of him."

Thirty Five

Evan

Thursday
10:05 pm
24 hours, 44 minutes
until the falling

How do you tell your best friend she has
hours to live?

Or that you might be the one responsible?

I stopped digging and opened my mouth, but it hung empty and dry. If I'd been killing Roslings by making them wear rubrics, how had Henri caught the affliktion? She'd never worn the rubrics —

You let her hold the clanker, remember?

No, it can't be. The skull will show us the truth. I'll prove Mazol is the murderer. Or Dravus. I haven't blacked out since —

You were asleep for hours today.

I was locked to the staircase.

You undid the shackles.

I pushed my shovel deep into the mud, pulling clod after dripping clod from the earth. Brown, sticky sod, like blood. The rain poured down. A vision appeared in the mud. It spread, snaking up my legs and the trees and the sky until it enveloped me.

Dravus drove his old rickety cart through the castle gates into the jungles. In the cart's bed lay a splintered wooden crate with clumps of mud and dirt clinging to its side. A gravebox, large enough to hold two or three, freshly dug from the ground. It rattled. Someone was inside, someone who wasn't dead.

I stood in the cart, staring down at the gravebox. The lid lifted with a moan. Pearl lay face up with lifeless eyes, staring at me, dwarfed by the oversized box. Under her torn dress, a scarlet rash that covered her neck and arms. At her collarbone, in place of the skull pendant I'd given her, was a tattoo of a spider.

Pearl lurched at me, screaming. She scratched; her skin bled. "Take it back! I don't want it anymore!" I reached out, to stop her from hurting herself, but when I leaned forward she disappeared in a wisp of smoke. Losing my balance, I fell into the gravebox.

The lid slammed, closing me inside. I fought to escape. Panic rose in my chest. I couldn't see. I couldn't breathe.

A sense grew inside me that I was not alone. I used my hand to probe the dusky void. Something was there, smooth and cold like iced meat. Lightning flashed, filling the box through a crack.

Henri's face, inches from mine. Drained of blood, covered in rash. Her eyes snapped open. The lightning ceased; darkness enveloped us. But I could still see her eyes. Lit by flames from within.

Her lips parted, but they did not move as she spoke. "Look what you've done to me."

A thud—my shovel struck wood. I felt Henri staring at my back. Were her eyes still burning? The blood pumpery rubric pounded inside my pocket. I felt the gravebox lid, clearing off mud to find its edge. I pushed the shovel under and pried, ignoring the pain from Pearl's bite and the exhaustion and the fear of Henri's flaming eyes. With the creak of rusty nails, the lid cracked open. Pearl screamed.

I was right.

A glow flickered in the distance. An oil lantern bobbed through the longgrass.

"Who's there?" Pearl said.

"It's me, Evan."

Shadows flashed across the tree limbs above us. Then voices. I turned to Henri. "Hide!" She darted behind the balizia's gnarled trunk. The screaming Shades at the gate rose in pitch. I peeked over the mound of dirt. Two shadows approached.

"Where am I?" Pearl said.

I crouched low. "Quiet. Someone's coming."

Rain pounded in my ears. Thunder clapped in the distance. I strained to hear, surprised to find I could make out the voices over the storm and the screaming Shades.

"I thought that was the plan," said the first. Yesler.

"Do you have any idea how much danger we're in?" said the second voice—Mazol. "If we're here when Cevo comes, if he finds all the Roslings cold and stiff and then he sees we're planning to make off with the ember and the Spider and the money?"

"Cevo don't know about Evan Burl. He don't know Terillium hid the gimp here."

"But he wants that Spider bad. He'll find it eventually. And when he does, he'll figure out we've been working him and Terillium against each other." Mazol's shadow turned, moving a step in my direction. They each had shovels.

"The automatons will activate soon," Yesler said. "Why don't we just execute the gimp and run?"

"We're lucky that syringe didn't kill him." A thunder clap rang out, shaking the ground. I strained to hear their voices over the downpour, but even with my heightened senses, I was having difficulty.

"He's gonna slit our throats if we don't do him first."

"Evan Burl is our only chance of seeing the summer with our heads still attached to our shoulders. We can trade him to Terillium or Cevo in exchange for our lives."

"You're dancing with death, keeping the gimp alive, that's what I say."

"We're immanis deeper in than that. The Cultures are coming. I can feel it."

I found the shovel and crawled over to the gravebox. Something seemed to be growing warm in my pocket.

"So what are we gonna do with the gimp?" Yesler said, "if he goes crazy on us?"

I pushed the shovel under the lid of the gravebox and heaved.

"Ballard's got the cage, in case it comes to that. And we've got the automatons."

Footsteps approached. The lid lifted a half inch and I forced the shovel head in further.

"Almost there Pearl," I whispered.

I pried on the lid again. The heat in my pocket burned my leg. I yanked out the leather sack of rubrics. My wet fingers sizzled. The sack fell into a puddle at my feet. The water bubbled and steamed and hissed.

"What's that noise?" Mazol said. I stomped at the bag, trying to bury it in the mud. The water frothed; the hissing fell to a simmer. A pulsing dusk rose from the gravebox's lid. Shadows grew deeper around us. Bubbling water around my feet exploded. The leather sack shot out of the water. Mazol's lantern flickered, like its energy was being pulled to the grave. A shape rose from the gravebox—the skull pendant and necklace. It passed straight through the lid. The necklace slid into the sack like a snake into a hole.

The leather sack floated above me. I pictured the book lifting from the fire. Holding out my hand, I tried to draw the rubrics to me. Feet sloshed through the mud toward me. A rat crawled over my foot. I kicked it away. When I looked up, the leather sack was gone. Pulling an old cart, Ballard lumbered behind Yesler and Mazol drawing toward me. I pushed the shovel between the lid and the gravebox and threw my weight on the handle. Two nails popped loose with a snap.

"What's going on here?" Yesler said.

I gaped up. The crate rattled. Pearl screamed. Ballard appeared, plucked me up by my shirt, threw me at Mazol's feet. I rose. His eyes drifted to something behind me. Yesler and Ballard's necks craned back as they gawked, higher and higher.

I spun around. Pearl's gravebox hovered above us. She thrashed inside, beating the wooden planks. With a crack, the gravebox exploded. She screamed. Debris fell around us. And where the gravebox once lay— a body, wrapped in a white sheet and straight as a pole. But why didn't she fall?

It's me.

I destroyed the gravebox. I'm holding her in the air.

She wobbled. Her body dropped. Taking one painful step, I leaped over the grave hole, catching her in my outstretched arms. We crashed to the ground on the far side. My back thudded against the balizia tree.

The world continued to roll. I crawled to Pearl. Ballard's hands clasped around our arms, dragged us through the mud, threw us both into the cage. Iron bars slammed down. A dozen giant birds took to the air, cawing and crashing through the branches above us. I pulled Pearl into my arms. Her chest heaved, her eyes flickered but didn't open.

I wrapped my fingers around the thick cell bars and pulled at them. Dizziness struck me. Henri stood in the shadows, rubrics in hand. She fumbled with the leather satchel at her side. My mind fell deeper into a fog. I felt my shoulder, the wound Pearl left me with, and now we were locked in a cage together.

My eyes drooped. I shook my head to stay awake. The villain was fighting for control of me. If Pearl attacked again, I'd have no choice. I'd be forced to kill her.

My head fell forward. I jerked it back, slapping my face.

Could I use sapience to become someone else? Anyone but me. Anywhere but here. I thought about the letter from Claire. My sister.

Where are you Claire? Will you trade lives with me?

And as I gave in to the dreams, I became someone else. I became my sister.

Thirty Six

Claire

Orange, dragon tongue flames licked up to
the ceiling, racing from the bed to the far
side of the room.

The door swung open. Someone had been in the room while our backs were turned.

And in my mind, I saw Ani unlock the door.

Something in the hall exploded, throwing me backward. I hit my head; my ears rang. Hot fog rolled along the floor in slow moving stream. I didn't see Anastasia. I felt for her in the bed of smoke. Shards of glass from the broken mirror scattered as I swept my hands along the floor. I thought I felt a dagger. The ebony blade. But it was just a splinter of wood. I heard laughing in the hall, my sister's voice. I crawled to the door. Flames walled me in.

"Ani!"

"I'm here," she said, sobbing behind me by the window.

I ran to her, leaned out into the cold night air. "Help!"

Hundreds of heads turned to us. Someone screamed. The whole courtyard burst into a sea of motion. Papa dashed to the nearest door, pushing anyone aside who didn't get out of his way.

From our window, I could see the other wings of our house. Sparks flickered in some of the windows. How could it have spread so fast? Unless someone had planned this? I saw my reflection in a bay of windows across the courtyard. Above me, flames crept up the roof. Anastasia screamed again and again. I might have slapped her if it wasn't for Terisma. She might push me out the window.

Billows of opaque fog and heat forced us to crawl onto a ledge. Cool to the touch but growing warm, plastered stone walls now stood between us and the flames. Inches from my face, a red beetle scrambled out onto the wall. Tiny wings appeared, carrying the bug away into the night.

Swirling pillars of smoke poured from the room next to us, but then changed directions and began to draw back inside. Anastasia edged further down the ledge, ebbing into a cloud of smoke. I thought I saw wings unfurl from her back. Huge raven wings. I tried to follow her, but the ledge was too broken for me to find footing.

"Hey!" I called. "Come back."

She didn't answer. My gut wrenched.

"Ani!"

Could she have fallen? Or flown away? "Where are you?" I yelled.

I stared back into the room and thought I caught a glimpse of the black knife laying on the floor. Smoke enveloped the room and poured out the window. I coughed. A breeze blew past. Anastasia appeared, edging along the ledge back to me. No wings on her back.

"You unlocked the door," I yelled, "didn't you?"

Below us, two men leaned a ladder against the wall. One of the men scrambled up the ladder, but the top was still a full ten feet below us. "More help is coming," he yelled.

"Get a longer ladder idiot!" Anastasia yelled. But the ladders — I had a horrible feeling they were gone. This was planned. Someone had taken them away. Burned them all days ago. I saw an image of the ladders burning. And the shadow watching.

"The ladders are missing —" The man was cut short by a ball of embers exploding from the room below us. He blew backward; flames licked up with scorching heat, singeing the hem of my dress. The man streaked through the air like one of Papa's fireworks. My foot slipped, and I fought to keep my grip on the crumbling wall. The man's body hit the ground on the far side of the courtyard, colliding with three others. Fire engulfed all four. Unnatural charring heat. They rolled on the ground, yelling as other men and women beat them with wet sacks. This pyre seemed unstoppable.

The flames that fed on the dying men leapt to another victim. She too fell to the ground screaming. Those who had been trying to beat out the fire jumped back, forming a ring. Safely distant. I watched two men hold a woman back from helping. After the victims had turned to motionless lumps, the flames continued to burn, feasting on the bodies until nothing remained but ash. I spotted a few people running down the hill away from the house. Others looked to follow. A breeze blew through the courtyard, carrying away our hope of survival. Those who stayed stared up at us, quiet and still as the perishing.

"Let me go!" Mother yelled. Her voice cut across the silent courtyard. "My family's in there!"

"You'll kill yourself."

"They need me!"

Smoke stung my eyes. It smelled sweet and sickening like too much sugar. Through slits, I watched her strain against three men. Thrashing and wriggling, she broke free, disappeared into the house. Would Mother find the shiv before the shadow? I imagined my hand wrapped around the blade. I should have taken it. But I couldn't. I couldn't do what Papa told me to do.

He should have found us by now; he might already be dead.

Or maybe Papa wasn't coming. What if he set the blaze himself, to create a distraction? He might have scorched the ladders too. I was the only one who knew about Evan Burl. If I died, there would be no one left to stop Papa.

"Do something!" Anastasia yelled to the crowd through desperate sobs. "Why aren't you trying to save us?" The people shook their heads, wiped their eyes, and stuffed their hands in their pockets.

An explosion rumbled through the building. The north wing toppled in a cloud of dust. The wall I clung to was starting to burn my hands. I began to wonder which was the worse way to die: roasting alive or falling.

I thought of the dream. Is this how it begins? Is it real this time?

The building shook again. My knees gave out. I slipped, clutched a ledge of rock, banged my knee, but was able to crawl back onto the ledge. I watched a wall to my right turn to pudding. A moment later, it was gone.

I gazed into Anastasia's eyes. "What do you think happens when we die?"

She didn't answer.

I wanted to say sorry for fighting with her. I pictured the wedding I'd always imagined. Having children. Two boys; I was sure boys would be easier than girls to raise—all of that was gone now... unless I learned to fly. The dream repeated again and again in my mind. The falling.

"Let's jump," I said.

"It's too far."

"Hold my hand."

She pulled away, out of reach. "Don't touch me."

"We'll burn alive if we don't do something."

"I can't jump."

"But what if—" It was useless, she didn't believe. But should I try without her? The wall I clung too began to shake. Plaster broke off in my hand and crumbled into salt. I closed my eyes and tried to concentrate. Learn to fly.

A crack shuddered through the house, into my bones. The narrow ledge I stood on disintegrated. I peered down. For the moment it took to breathe a single gasp, I stood on nothing but air. Just as my body sank into the fall, something seized my hand. "Papa!"

He hoisted me like I weighed no more than a fire-lantern. My toes found solid footing. Balancing, I clung to the wall as he adjusted his grip on my hands. The cuts on my hands stung.

"Save me first!" Anastasia screamed. She pushed me, causing my hand to slip from Papa's. I fell backward. My fingers slipped into a crack in the wall, saving me from tumbling into the smoke below. Screams from the onlookers.

"Careful," Papa said.

He reached for me again. My knees shook. I couldn't bring myself to pull my fingers from the crack.

"Everything's going to be alright," Papa said. "I promise."

"What about the fire?"

He glanced behind him. "A little tinder like this? I've survived worse." He smiled.

"But what about the knife? I didn't touch it. I swear. I left it on the desk. The shadow must have taken it."

"Calm down child."

But Ani unlocked the door. She let the shadow in. I pictured Sophia as Ani and I ran down the stairs this morning. "We've been waiting a long time for this," she said. "Don't forget what I told you." She whispered in my ear, like I knew what she meant. But I didn't. How could I have known what she meant? She must have been talking to Ani. They were planning something. I wanted to scream at Ani. *What did Sophia mean? What are you planning with her?* But I said nothing. I willed myself to pull one hand from the crack, stretching up as Papa reached for me. His eyes flashed to my belt, then back to my face. The book. Or did he look at my hand? My empty hand?

His eyes narrowed at me. "What are you doing?"

"I didn't mean to take it."

He wanted the book, maybe more than me. Maybe more than his life. He was going to let me fall, once he had the book in his hands.

"What are you waiting for?" Ani screamed.

Flames and smoke rolled from the window; I imagined a fireshark thrashing inside Ani's room. Papa's forehead was dry, not a drop of sweat. I jumped for his hand. My fingertips grasped his, but my skin was too wet and I slipped. I slid back until my feet found the ledge again.

The wall shuddered. I gazed into Papa's eyes. My stomach turned inside out. I wanted to hurt him. No, just to tell him to leave Evan Burl alone; to curse at him for hurting me; to say goodbye.

"Something came over the wall," I shouted. "It's in the house. A shadow. I think it got your dagger—"

"If you won't go," Anastasia said, "I will." She tried to step around me. I slipped.

Papa pointed to a metal bar that jutted out from the wall. "Grab that!"

I barely caught hold of it. Finding my balance, I said, "What about Ani? Save her first."

"Not now Claire. Just do as you're told."

Ani's eyes burned. Terisma wanted to play. I gazed down at the sea of faces below, for a moment, I felt like we were acting in a play. They would cry soon, shed a tear when I fell to my death. Then they would go home talking about what a wonderful performance it was. I could play three characters all at once.

"Jump," Papa said. "I'll catch you."

I reached on my toes, but he was too far away. "I can't."

"Trust me. Jump."

I closed my eyes. My body grew airy, ghostly. Maybe I was dead. My feet had nothing but air below them, but I wasn't falling. I was flying. Papa lifted me with magic. Putting my hand in his, I rose. I saw over the ledge. A glimpse of the ebony blade, laying on the window ledge. I had never touched it. Not once. I remembered how it stuck out of the desk; its tip jabbed into the ebony wood. How did it get in here? The shadow? I was almost through the window when Papa's face changed.

I felt my weight return to me in a rush. "I'm slipping!"

My hand slid from his and I fell. My arms were just able to wrap around the window sill as my body slammed into the wall. Papa's face drained of blood, his eyes rolled backward. Staggering back, he turned away from me. When he faced me again, a pulsing blade stuck from the center of his chest, eyeless and midnight. The knife.

Smoke filled the room. I couldn't see who was behind him.

"You?" he said. "Why..."

"Papa!" I yelled. Blood soaked his torn shirt.

His eyes found mine. "The book," he said through gasps, "You must..."

He coughed. Blood dripped from his lips. Sparks and flame engulfed him. "Make sure Mazol..." He coughed blood again. "If he fails... you must..."

"What?" I said. "What should I do?"

"Trust me, Claire."

"I do," I said.

"I love you... little Bell. No matter what you've done. Even after this."

"I shouldn't have taken the book. I'm sorry. I'll do whatever you ask."

"Execute Evan Burl—" He collapsed. A moment later, Mother appeared, her clothes and skin charred, but somehow she had managed to survive the blaze. She gazed with stone eyes at Papa lying on the floor. I saw blood on her hands. But what about the shadow? Could Mother be working with it? Could Mother be the shadow?

Mother had been arguing with Papa. Sophia. The shadow. Ani. They all knew something I didn't. Like they were planning something. Something horrible. And somehow, Papa knew. He had planned for this. That's why he let me find out about Evan Burl. He wanted me to make sure the job was done after he was gone.

Stepping over Papa's body, her eyes found us.

"Claire!" She rushed to the window.

"Don't touch me," I said.

"Help me then!" Anastasia screamed.

Mother ignored Ani and reached under my arms, but her hands were slippery with blood. A beam broke free from the ceiling and landed on Mother's back. Crumpling to the ground, she caught fire. Flames raced through her lacy evening dress, catching in her perfect golden hair. She screamed.

The whole building began to shake. Anastasia appeared at the window. How did she get into the room?

"You pushed past when Mother was trying to save me," I said.

"You always loved that you were their favorite," she said. The flames licked up her back. She didn't scream. The bracelet on her arm pulsed slate and dusk, inhaling gleam from the flames.

"You should have made Papa save me first," she said.

"Help me up, Ani."

"We're all going to die. Someday." She seized my wrists. "You first." She threw me backward. And as I fell, I glimpsed Papa floating in the middle of the inferno. Then, an explosion.

It started inside him, right where the dagger pierced his chest. An earthquake erupted. Yet, no sound. Beginning with his body, everything around him—walls, chest-of-drawers, carved stone statues, glass—even light, was pulled to that single point. An exploding star in reverse. I blew backward on a wave of rays, just outside the explosion's grasping fingers.

It almost felt like I was floating on a pillow of thin air.

Propelled by the explosion's force, a ship riding the crest of a wave; I plunged into the smoky fog that rose from the earth. What was left of Anastasia's room disintegrated into dust as a shockwave blew out from my Papa's chest. The book lifted from my pocket, floating away just out of my grasp.

Something fell above me. Papa. The explosion was just light, his body had been spared. He was alive. Barely.

"Evan Burl," I whispered, "I've been talking to him with the book. He asked me about the falling."

"Break the vialus and you will see the falling for yourself."

My hand found the trinket on my wrist, the one shaped like an hourglass.

"How do I break it?"

I saw the world rushing up reflected in Papa's eyes.

"Let me." He snapped his fingers. A vialus appeared. He pushed it at me, it bounced off my chest. The glass burst. A sound like sucking wind and crackling lightning. Smoke curled out in wisps, but it was carried upward by the heat of the pyre. It burrowed into Papa. And none was left for me.

His eyes filled with horror. "No!"

The clear midnight sky, like a jacket wrapped around the world, unzipped itself, revealing a coral sunset beyond. A second setting sun pierced the darkness like streams of red glow through broken clouds. Rushing wind yanked at his bones, his skin turned to vapor. Then he was taken away, sucked into the night as the distant world closed around him.

I opened my mouth to scream, but no sound came out. The ground rushed up at me, too fast to escape. Squeezing my eyes shut, I realized this isn't how the dream begins. This is how it ends.

This is how I killed Claire Amadeus.

Thirty Seven

Evan

Friday
5:35 pm
5 hours, 14 minutes
until the falling

"Is it possible, I mean, do you think
you're my sister?"

A mocking voice rang in my ears. The sound struck my head like a pry bar. I sat up. The world lurched sideways. I couldn't focus past the thick rusted bars that surrounded me. I tried to remember the dream I'd just been pulled from. The falling was different this time—I saw my father above me. And then, at the end, I died.

"I want to help you," Yesler said, "I'm trying to stop Papa from hurting you."

Yesler was reading my conversation with Claire. A face leered down at me. I squinted my eyes. Yesler emerged from the blur. I grabbed through the bars. He held the book out of my reach.

"Good thing your daddy had the sense to make a coop for freaks like you."

Through the pounding in my head, other sounds became clear. Grinding gears of the finishing clanker. Hissing of the boiler's steam pipes. Roaring of the furnace.

I threw my weight against the bars.

Yesler grinned. "No one can bend 'em. Not even you."

There must be a way out, a door to open, a lock to unbolt, but my mind felt only emptiness. My sapience was gone. Missing. With a pain in my chest, I remembered who sat in the cage with me. I turned slowly around. Pearl leaned against the bars, eyes closed, so near she could strangle me if she just reached out her hands. My heart went cold.

"Took Ballard all day to pull this coop from the dungeon. Guess we don't have to worry about you no more."

I reached out with my mind, trying to twist Yesler's neck. My head swam, pulsing with burning pain. I gripped the bars to keep from falling over.

Yesler bared his teeth through the hole in his mask. "Can't do your tricks no more, can you?"

The cage was robbing me of sapience. Yesler disappeared. I slumped against the bars. The real world faded in and out with the rhythm of a grinding belt. I closed my eyes and concentrated; someone was watching me. I looked at Pearl and thought I saw her eyes snap shut.

I forced my eyes shut again, felt inside the bars with my mind—my skull pounding—and traced them, one by one. No cracks, no seams. I reached with my hands, heaving the bars apart. Cakes of rust crumpled off. My brain screamed, my forehead broke with sweat, but the bars didn't budge.

I thought you weren't using sapience.

A voice startled me. "Evan."

I pushed my face against the cage. A face swam from the blur.

"Henri?"

"Shhh."

The roof seemed to be crushing down on top of me. I pushed my hands against it. "You're still alive! The affliktion—"

"Don't worry about that."

She started to evaporate into the fog. I thrust my hand through the bars and grabbed her wrist. "Wait! Last night. You had a rash—"

She shook her head. I tried to focus on her but couldn't see well enough to be sure. Had I imagined it all? "What about the skull?"

She hesitated. "Mazol took it."

"You gave it to him?"

"He said he'd kill you if I didn't. For what it's worth, you were right about Pearl...." She clutched my hand through the bars then whispered, "remember who you are. You're good. They're going to try to make you think terrible things." She glanced over her shoulder. "I have to go."

Henri's hand slid out of mine, and she melted into the blurry fog that surrounded me. I heard the sound of fabric scraping against bronze. Pearl shifted. A rush of voices hit me like a wall, one rising, another falling.

"Watch the brakes," someone said.

"You're late," said another.

"I had to take the long way."

"Evan's crate is blocking the stairs."

I couldn't be sure if they were really talking at the same time, or talking at all. Maybe I was dreaming.

"You said you would let him go," Henri said.

A murmur came in reply—my uncle?—but too clouded to understand.

"He's not well," she said. "I think he's dying."

Someone answered—the voice belonged to Mazol—but I couldn't hear his words.

"I'm not doing this anymore," she said.

I swallowed. My ears popped.

"You'll do as you're told," Mazol said.

"You're not keeping your end of the deal."

A chorus of other voices flooded the conversation, making it impossible to hear what Henri and Mazol said next.

"Take it, quick!" someone yelled.

"Not that high, not that high."

"All right, done up here."

"Keep it moving."

The voices got louder and louder until my head wanted to break. I curled into a ball, my hands pressed over my ears. "Stop!" I yelled aloud. Everything went silent.

Lowering my hands, I listened, searching for Henri. Slowly, her voice grew in my mind.

"He's starting to figure it out," Henri said.

"You better make sure he don't," Mazol said.

"What if I can't"

"It'll be the belt for you, and worse for him."

Other voices crowded in.

"Do you see that?"

"Something is up there."

"What are you all staring at?" Mazol yelled.

"It's falling," someone said, also not in my head.

"Look, through the ceiling."

"It's getting bigger."

I pulled myself to the bars. Everything became clear. Mazol and Henri stood fifty feet away at the top of a staircase. Ravenna and Gertrude and others leaned over handrails; Parkrose and Vashion stood in the center of the room; all stared up at the glass ceiling. Ballard and Yesler had stopped to see what the others were looking at.

I heard movement behind me. Pearl. One of her eyes flittered. I turned back to the sky, past the blazing furnace, past the lake-sized Caldroen filled with boiling water, past the six levels of walkways and balconies filled with clankers, past dozens of nickel spiral staircases, all the way to the expansive glass dome that capped the hollow tower and to the painted sky beyond.

An orange blotch sparkled. My eyes lost focus. Staggering, I fell against the bars. The room plunged into a muffled quiet, like my head had been dipped underwater. The clankers spluttered to the point of explosion, yet the machines made no noise.

Incomprehensible shouts broke through the clogged silence. I stared up, blinded by light. Sight came and went. Ravenna shielded her eyes. Roxhill backed against the wall. Their mouths moved, but their voices came later, like thunder rolling a long breath after lightning strikes.

"Watch out!"

A deafening crash reverberated through my body, splitting my vision into two blurry images that danced before me. They snapped together; I saw clearly. The glass ceiling imploded.

Through it, fell a girl.

Glass rained down, striking each level of the iron walkway. I jumped on Pearl to shield her from the glittering razors until the downpour ended.

I peered up. The girl was still falling.

Her long silver hair floated as if underwater. Her body made billowing waves through the dusty air. Her dress flickered with flames, reflecting the burnt orange sky. I thought she might be flying. If I could fly like that, I might have saved Pike.

She collided with the boiler, where the tank bulged out like a fat man's belly. I winced, expecting her frail body to bounce off the cast bronze walls. But she went straight through, like the double-wall encasements were made of paper.

Supports burst, iron twisted, the girl cut through everything in her path. I caught glimpses of her through the furnace's vents. Even the flames seemed not to touch her.

The tower groaned and tipped toward us. The boiler on top shuddered. Supports caved. The boiler rocked, then fell. An avalanche of water and twisted bronze and nickel tumbled down.

Vashion and Haller dove under a clanker. Gertrude and Othella dashed out of the Caldroen. The Warts found cover under an overhanging ledge. I heaved against the cage's bars. My hand slipped, slamming my elbow. I tried again. One of the bars creaked. My head burst with pain. A dragonfly hovered next to my ear; I heard each beat of its wings.

Bracing myself against the corner, I pushed the bent bar with my leg. It twisted. I pushed again. The bar groaned. I kicked again and again and again. It shattered. The dragonfly floated away. I wriggled through. With slippery fingers, I grasped Pearl's hand. She jerked awake, her eyes wild.

I pulled her through the gap, then holding her to my side, I jumped. Catching the rail of the level above us, I swung us both under an overhanging ledge just as the water crashed down. It hit with a clap of thunder and a sea of brick and stone and chrome.

I rolled onto my back, and my chest heaved. But the headaches, the throbbing pain, the swimming mind—gone. I watched Mazol and others appear on different levels above us, leaning over the rails, gaping at the scene. Water rushed out of the broken wall into the courtyard, leaving behind a tangle of steel spider skeletons and iron snakes and oaken brambles. The cage was flat as stomped tin.

Lying at the peak of the bramble mountain: the girl. Her dress, untorn. Her silver hair, combed and straight. Her skin, without blemish. A raven black chain around her wrist caught my eye.

I jumped down, landed knee deep in water, crawled up the pile of wreckage. Mazol ascended from the other side. We reached the top together. His eyes drifted to the dark chain. I thought he might reach for it when a shape appeared.

A man. He slumped beside the girl, wearing a long leather coat. The tip of an onyx blade stuck out his back, the handle protruded from his chest, blood dripping from its edge. He stooped over—half falling, half kneeling—and spoke into the girls ear.

"Terillium?" Mazol said.

The man peered up. His eyes scanned past me to Mazol, then back to me. He straightened his back. Staggered toward me, his hands out like he might embrace me. Or strangle me.

I felt myself shrink under him. "Father?"

Thirty Eight

Terillium

Friday
5:40 pm
5 hours, 9 minutes
until the falling

I stared at Evan Burl.

Aperti sunt oculi mei. I might have been looking at a younger version of myself. I opened my mouth, but found no words.

My eyes wandered. The Caldroen. The apparatuses, what was left of them. Just like I'd left this place so many years ago, like I'd stepped through time. Like everything had been frozen in a sheet of ice, just waiting for me to arrive. To bring it back to life.

Several girls stared at me. *The children*. My head oscillated like I'd finished a bottle of 1292 all on my own.

"Cevo wanted to slaughter them..." My voice slurred. I felt like one of those people who can't stand silence, people who fill the uncomfortable quiet with things that shouldn't be said. "But I wouldn't stand for it. I made him send them here." Or maybe I saw the way Evan looked at me. Abhorrence mingled with disquietude. "I knew he'd never look for you where he sent the girls. It was all so impeccable."

"You're hurt." Evan came to me. I leaned over him, smelled his hair. Below us, Claire slept. I'd placed too much on her shoulders. Any child would have fractured under such an encumbrance. Anyone. She would be better once I was gone. She was tenacious.

And Evan Burl? He seemed suddenly innocuous. I wondered if I had been wrong about him. I should have kept him out of this. If I'd just let him live a natural life. "The Spider? Do you have it?"

"I-I don't know what you mean."

I found Mazol. "Brother? Where is the Spider? Bring it to me quickly."

"It's gone."

"And the ember?" I said to Mazol.

"It was just like you foretold. Cevo arranged everything."

"I must have it now."

Mazol hesitated.

"It could save my life." I collapsed next to Claire.

Mazol ran from the room; I had a feeling he would not return. Evan crouched next to me. I put my hand on his face. Blood marred his cheek.

"Take care of Claire. Tell her I was wrong."

"But the falling—"

"Tell her I still love her. And that, I must go away for a while, but it's not forever. We'll see each other again."

"You told Mazol to kill me."

"Yes. I did."

"And now you want me to help you?"

"I was afraid. I don't know what to make of you Evan Burl."

"So you just left me here?"

"I thought you might grow up strong enough to use the Spider, to rule the Cultures when I was gone, to ensure that sapience lives on un-abused. Cevo would have done anything for the Spider. I knew this was the one place he'd never look." I felt my face crack from smiling and fell into a fit of coughing.

"You didn't have to leave me."

"You're lucky to be alive. If I'd known what I know now, I'd have smothered you while you still slept in your mother's womb." Talking lacerated my lungs. I had to stop. I had to breathe.

"How can you say that?"

"It would have been mercy. Sapience is growing; I can't explain it. My brothers and I required decades to master the easiest of tasks, to make an orange hover above our hand or to crush a flower without touching it. I've seen people do more with just weeks of practice now. And you, the most powerful of all, I feared sapience would tear you to pieces." I couldn't feel my legs. Death crawled through my bones, searching for my defenseless heart to squeeze until it beat no more. It's felicitous, I suppose. Ironic maybe, that I will die in Evan's arms, like his mother died in mine. Requiescant in pace.

"Isn't there any hope?"

"In honesty, no. I stand by what I wrote to your uncle. I still believe you will become an abomination. I think you will bring harm to your own friends and much, much worse. But I yearn to be wrong."

"You came to kill me."

"I never wanted to see you, I knew it would make my choice too difficult to bear. And now I can see I was right. It's easy Evan—you'll understand this if you live long enough to walk my path—but it's easy to order the execution of someone with whom you've never shared a glass of wine or felt the warmth of his presence flowing through his veins." I coughed again, felt blood drool down by chin.

Evan was silent. Claire didn't move. The other girls stared. I put my hand on his chest. "Be strong Evan Burl. I have the faintest glimmer of hope that I'm still wrong about you."

"But—"

"I won't say I'm sorry for leaving you here. But I will say this: prove me wrong."

Evan Burl stared at me as the room faded into darkness. I thought he would speak, either to hurt or to comfort, but he did neither. In the dim light, I think he began to understand me more than he would have liked. If anyone could understand me fully—in only the way that a son and sire can know each other—it was Evan Burl. The reflection of candle light in his bright eyes was the final vision to enter my senses as my heavy lids fell. Death wrapped its fingers around my heart. My frozen body didn't have the strength to shiver. My lips parted for their final words. I said what my sire said to me before he slept for the last time, what Evan Burl might have said to me, had he lived another life instead of the one I forced upon him.

"My blood for yours. Haec ego in te... I live on in you."

Thirty Nine

Evan

Friday
5:49 pm
5 hours until the falling

My Father faded.

No, he melted; like a water painting in the rain. The lines between where he began and where he ended blurred until parts of him became unrecognizable. The blade that pierced his chest turned to dripping globs of molten chrome until it had all seeped into the mountain of debris we stood on.

His face remained last, confusion and regret written in the lines on his forehead. His jaw stuttered, but no more words came. Then he was gone.

"I live on in you." His words made me warm and cold in waves. And his accent? The same as Henri's. Mazol and Yesler appeared at a door.

"It's too late," I said. "He's gone."

"You stay where you are gimp," Yesler said. He and Mazol climbed the mound.

Henri followed behind them, her fingers twitching on the satchel at her side. "Just do what they say and everything will be alright."

I lifted my hand.

"Don't move." Yesler snagging Henri from behind, pressed a razor to her skin. She fought him. I stretched my fingers; the shiv flew from Yesler's hand into mine. I pointed it at Yesler. He put his hands into the air. Henri stumbled back.

"Here's what's gonna happen," I said. "I want to know what's been happening to the Roslings. I want the skull. I want the Spider. I want whatever you were going to get for my Father—the ember. And I want it now."

I like this new you.

Mazol glanced at Henri.

The steel lifted from my hand, floating point first toward him. "I don't have much practice; I don't know if I'll be able to stop it."

He looked at Henri again. She fumbled with the satchel, slipping something out. I lost my concentration on the knife; it fell at Mazol's feet with a clank. Lunging, he twisted me by the ear. "I don't take no orders from no gimp."

I tried to push him away but couldn't think straight. A pendent hung from Mazol's neck. I'd never seen it before: a mechanized girl with burning red eyes. I imagined her staring at me, eating up my sapience, like the cage. A rubric made for protecting its wearer from the attack of people like me. I swung at Mazol. Missed. An oil-soaked beam rose into the air and exploded. I shielded my face from the splinters.

Mazol whispered in my ear. "She's going to get you."

"Shut up."

"She'll stab you in the back."

"She'd never..." But I felt only half as convinced of Henri's innocence as I sounded. I watched Henri, searching for signs of her guilt. Could she hurt me? Could she have hurt the Roslings? She stood next to Yesler, in her hand the object she had pulled from her satchel: a syringe, filled with murky dusk. She put a single finger to her lips, tested the plunger with her thumb. Three drops fell from the tip. Henri was going to stick Mazol in the back. She would prove her love for me, just as Mazol was trying to convince me of her guilt.

She raised the syringe above her head. Yesler tried to grab it from her. She pushed him off, more easily than I thought possible. Mazol didn't see; his eyes were locked on me. I had distrusted Henri—even if only for a moment. But it was more than that. I'd accused her of turning on me, of siding with Mazol. I'd even, if I was honest with myself deep down, accused her of murdering the Roslings. I had wanted it to be anyone but me. Even if that meant my best friend took my place.

I held my breath as her hand fell. Yesler lunged at her. They both fell toward me as the syringe came down in an arc.

Mazol turned. "No!"

But she didn't stab Mazol. She reached past him. Her eyes never left me. The tip of the needle plunged deep into the muscle between my shoulder and neck. Yesler grinned. Blood oozed from his cracked lips, dripping down the white mask. I staggered backward and grasped for the syringe. It fell, bursting at my feet. Someone screamed.

I fell next to Claire, my body sprawled in the puddle of my father.

To be continued.

Thank you for reading
Evan Burl and the Falling, Vol. 1-2!

Download a FREE copy of Vol. 3 and keep reading Evan's tale now
www.justinblaney.com/vol3

Or, you can purchase Vol. 3 wherever fine ebooks are sold. Links to all the most
popular stores can be found here: www.justinblaney.com/vol3

Please consider helping others discover Evan's world by reviewing this book on
Amazon or your favorite bookseller. You can earn signed copies of any my books by
sending me links to your reviews.
Find out more at www.justinblaney.com/reviews-are-beautiful

And I'd love to hear from you! Stay in touch by email at justin@justinblaney.com
Or connect on social media @justinblaney

Your friend, Justin